COLT

COLT

Nancy Springer

Dial Books for Young Readers

NEW YORK

Published by
Dial Books for Young Readers
A Division of Penguin Books USA Inc.
375 Hudson Street
New York, New York 10014

Library of Congress Cataloging in Publication Data
Springer, Nancy.
Colt / by Nancy Springer.
p. cm.
Summary: A young boy with a crippling disease learns,
through a horseback riding program, to overcome his own anxieties
and to help others in dealing with their own problems.
ISBN 0-8037-1022-4 (trade)
[1. Physically handicapped—Fiction. 2. Horsemanship—Fiction.
3. Horses—Fiction.] I. Title.
PZ7.S76846Co 1991 [Fic]—dc20 90-20693 CIP AC

For Carmin Daryman,
with great appreciation,
and for
Anne and Jack Wagner of Usin' Hoss Ranch,
and for
all handicapped kids everywhere,
and everyone involved with
Horseback Riding for the Handicapped.

Chapter One

"I don't want to!" Colt complained.

His therapist was patient with him, as usual. "Hey, c'mon, big guy, with a name like yours you should love horses."

Mrs. Berry, always nice, always cheery—she drove Colt nuts. He raised his voice to a bombshell whine. "I don't! And you can't make me. I hate this place. It stinks." The stable smelled of horses and saddles, sawdust and manure. Strong, warm smells. Colt did not in fact mind them, but he minded being brought to Deep Meadows Farm against his will. He whined, "I want to go home. Nobody asked me—"

"You're scared," taunted Neely Brenneman from farther up the stable aisle.

Colt knew quite well by the lizards crawling a-round in his stomach that it was true he was scared. This fact made him even angrier than Mrs. Berry's everlasting sweetness. It made him angry because he felt ashamed of his fear, and why should he? He had every right to be scared. So why wouldn't people let him be scared? He was not a "big guy." He was small for his age, and even if he wasn't, he felt small, because he was in a wheelchair looking up. When you're in a wheelchair, with people bending over you and trundling you around like a baby in a stroller, you feel small. And you feel scared, because when you have spina bifida, the bones in your legs are brittle, and if you bang against something you could break them. If you rub open the lump of spinal nerve tissue on your back, you could have to go to the hospital. If you hit the metal-and-plastic tube nestled in your brain, you could have to get operated on. Again.

"I am not scared!" he yelled at Neely. Though of course Neely knew he was. Colt felt scared of half the world and Neely knew, because Neely was in a wheelchair too. Neely had been born with a defect of the spine, just like Colt. Neely had a shunt hidden under his scalp too, and a soft plastic tube running down under the skin of his neck to take the excess fluid away from his brain. Neely had a lump on his back like Colt's. Neely couldn't use his legs either.

None of this made Colt like Neely any better. Neely was a real boogerhead.

"Neely," reproached Mrs. Berry, "we don't tease. Colt, here we go. Let's go meet your horse." Because he could not propel himself on the loose dirt of the stable aisle, she pushed his wheelchair toward the nearest stall. Colt grabbed for his brakes to stop her, but she just reached down and pushed his hands away. If she had to, she'd lift the whole wheelchair with him in it. He couldn't do a thing about it when Mrs. Berry took charge. Even yelling didn't help.

He yelled anyway, because Colt hated to give up. "No! I don't want to!" All up and down the stable aisle parents and aides and other grown-ups were pretending not to hear him, but he could see that they looked uncomfortable. Good, he thought. He hollered, "I don't like horses!"

Mrs. Berry ignored him. "Here's our first rider, Mrs. Reynolds," she said brightly to the blue-jeaned woman standing by the stall door. "Colt Vittorio."

Mrs. Reynolds nodded and did not bend over him or try to sweet-talk him or ask him if Colt was his real name. She had a no-makeup face and a slim, outdoorsy look, and she met his eyes in a man-to-man way. Okay, he thought. She seemed unaffected by the noise he was still making. *Not* okay.

"Colt," she said, "meet Liverwurst. Liverwurst, this is Colt."

A huge heavy-boned, long-nosed fleshy head swung out over the stall door and nodded in the air somewhere above Colt.

He gasped, trying to lean back and flinch away, though in a wheelchair he could do neither. He gawked, too stunned even to yell anymore. Liverwurst looked like a diseased, no, a *mutant* fungus crawling out of a horror-movie dark hole of a stall. Liverwurst was all speckles and blotches of liver-brown, yellow, and dirty white. His nose looked like a bad case of sunburn. His eyes reminded Colt of eggs fried too long, with greasy brown whites. And if Liverwurst's head was so big and ugly, the rest of him (hidden behind the stall door) had to be—

"Liverwurst is an Appaloosa," said the stable woman as if nothing was wrong.

The rest of him had to be monstrous beyond belief. Big heavy shoulders. Great leaping haunches. Huge, hard steel-shod hooves that could smash a kid with a single kick.

"Colt," Mrs. Berry directed, "feed him his treat."

Colt looked down to discover that his clammy hands, shaking in his lap, were clutching an apple. He did not remember how or when it had gotten there, but he knew he could blame it on Mrs. Berry.

The horse smelled the apple. Trying to reach it, Liverwurst swung his head low, so low Colt could whiff his hot sour breath and feel it stirring his hair. The horse's fleshy nose reached to just above Colt's head.

"Hold it up where he can get it, Colt!" Mrs. Berry urged.

Colt honestly couldn't move. It's one thing to be a regular person with legs that can take you away if something turns out to be dangerous, and it's another thing to be trapped in a wheelchair with a

gung-ho grown-up at the handles. Colt felt petrified.

Liverwurst nodded eagerly and snorted, flaring his
nostrils and spraying Colt with a polka-dot splatter-
ing of mud-brown horse snot.

"He won't hurt you," Mrs. Berry said. "All of Mrs.
Reynolds's horses are very gentle." Ah-ha—so she
was saying it was okay to be afraid of some horses!
And how did she know which ones? But before Colt
could point this out, Mrs. Berry grabbed his hands.
"This way," she directed, prying open his clenched
fingers and flattening them out so that the apple
perched on his palms.

The horse was starting to paw with anxiety to get
at the apple. Colt could hear a hoof, maybe about
the size of a manhole cover, thudding someplace inside the stall. Crack, crack against the thin wooden
wall between him and Colt—like the crack of doom.

"Hurry," said Mrs. Berry. "It's okay." Those two
concepts didn't seem to go together. Nevertheless,
Mrs. Berry guided Colt's hands up toward Liverwurst's straining, reaching nose. *It's not okay!* Colt
wanted to shout, but he couldn't. His chest had gone
tight. He was sweating and panting. He couldn't talk.

Liverwurst's mouth gaped open about six inches
in front of Colt's bugging eyes. Humongous rubbery
lips pulled back from yellow-stained teeth that were
as long as piano keys. In one powerful chomp Liverwurst bit the apple in half right through the core.

"Aaaaa!" Colt yelled. Screamed, really.

Liverwurst tossed his huge head (about the size and weight of a medium-small dog) and chewed vigorously. Apple juice and bits of squashed apple pulp frothed out from the corners of his mouth and flew into Colt's face.

"Oh, honestly, Liverwurst," the stable lady chided the horse.

Colt found his voice. "I don't like it. Make him stop! Get me away from him!" He was almost crying, and furious because he hated to cry when people could see him. It was embarrassing enough that he had screamed. Blast Mrs. Berry for getting him into a situation that made him want to cry.

"Eewww!" Colt protested as Liverwurst lowered his slobbering mouth for the rest of the apple. "No, I don't want to! I'm going to throw up!"

"I don't blame you," said Mrs. Reynolds, the stable lady. "Liverwurst is being disgusting." She took what was left of the apple out of Colt's hands and fed it to the horse, coaxing his big homely head away from Colt. "Liverwurst apologizes for forgetting his manners," she told Colt, "and thanks you for the treat." She was neither smiling nor not smiling. He could not tell if she was making fun of him. "Let me get the saddle and bridle on him, and you can ride him."

It was time to start all over again. Would these grown-ups never learn? "I don't want to!" shouted Colt.

Most of the people had emptied out of the stable aisle. The other handicapped riders had fed their apples to their horses, and volunteers had saddled the animals and led them outside to the mounting ramp. Neely was up at the top of the ramp, being helped out of his wheelchair and onto a perky gray pony named Giggles. Colt, Mrs. Berry, and Mrs. Reynolds were alone inside the stable, with Liverwurst of course.

Mrs. Berry squatted down in front of Colt. "Young man," she said, "I want to remind you that the director of the center is here tonight. Now, we don't want to give him a bad impression of our Horseback Riding for the Handicapped program, do we?"

Colt observed that Mrs. Berry had a small mustache, nearly invisible, on her upper lip. He watched it as she talked.

"Most of our horseback riders find the experience very rewarding."

Mrs. Berry also had a mole near her nose with a single brown hair curling out of it. The brown hair jiggled in time with the blond mustache on her lip.

"Horseback riding will be good for your back and legs. It exercises muscles you don't normally get to use."

"I don't care," said Colt. There was no chance he would ever walk without his crutches and heavy thigh-high braces, no matter how much they exercised his legs.

"Colt, you know what I think of that I-don't-care attitude."

A lot of the time Colt felt as if the real Colt was

far away, as if he not only had great running legs but could fly, as if he were really in the sky somewhere, outside everything, looking in. He felt that way now. Looking down, not only could he see Mrs. Berry and her mustache but also himself, a darkhaired boy, stubborn chin, chunky shoulders, small for his age, belted into a wheelchair and trapped in the dark stable aisle.

I don't care!

Because if he let himself care, how could he deal with the way he felt? He hated being handicapped. He hated having a shunt in his head and a lump on his back and not being able to walk and run like other kids. He hated spending half his life in doctors' offices and physical therapy and being fitted for braces. He hated costing his mother so much money that they never had enough for anything nice. He hated needing people to do things for him.

Mrs. Berry wanted him to be a good sport. And sure, he was cheerful sometimes, around Christmas for instance, but he saw no reason why he should ever be cheerful about his spina bifida. Especially not just to impress the director of the Easter Seals Center where he had his therapy. He didn't care about him either.

He said so, top volume. "I don't CARE. I don't WANT to ride a dumb horse. I just want people to LEAVE ME ALONE—"

"Colt," interrupted a quiet voice, "I want you to do me and Liverwurst a favor. I know he made a pig of himself about the apple; I know you don't like him much at this point, but I do want you to give him another chance, please. Let him show you what a good horse he is."

It was Mrs. Reynolds, and she had the saddle and bridle on the Appaloosa horse. She was leading him out of the stall, and he was every bit as big as Colt was afraid he was. His hocks passed at the level of Colt's face.

And ugly. He had a tail like a rat, nearly no hair on it. And on his thick neck only wisps of scraggly mane.

He clopped down the aisle like a big donkey, with his homely head nodding in a gentle way.

For half a moment Colt considered doing what Mrs. Reynolds asked, as a favor to her. He liked her plain weathered face and crinkled gray eyes and the level way she talked to him. And though it was hard to remember at the time, he did very much like horses, as long as people weren't trying to shove him into their big bony faces or onto their powerful backs. He owned several books about horses. He had taken a special interest in horses ever since he could remember, ever since his mother had nicknamed him Colt because something about his thin, useless legs reminded her of a newborn colt's spindly ones. He liked to watch shows on TV about horses.

Then again, he liked to watch shows about man-eating tigers too. "No. NO! I don't want to!"

But by that time Mrs. Berry had spun him around

and pulled him backward up the mounting ramp. And the director of the center was standing ready to help—smiling like a snake. And the two of them were lifting him out of his wheelchair.

Colt didn't want anyone ever to call him a quitter. Briefly he considered throwing a real fit, flailing his arms, hitting, maybe giving someone a black eye. But Mrs. Berry was wearing her most patient look. He knew if he tried a tantrum she would just hug his arms down and croon and cuddle him, and he despised being treated like a baby. And if he struggled while he was being lifted he might make her drop him; he might fall and hit his shunt and die. Nobody had ever told him that hitting his shunt might make him die, but he knew it could.

The others were on their way down to the riding ring. Anna Susanna, who had cerebral palsy, rode a white-faced strawberry roan. Matt, who was deaf, was on a chunky bay mare. Jay Gee, the retarded boy, had a big sand-colored dun. Neely rode the gray pony, Giggles. And cutesy-pie little Julie was on a tiny pinto-spotted Shetland pony with a shaggy mane. Julie had mild cerebral palsy and was such a sweet little angel face all the time, the kind you always see on TV shows about handicapped kids, she made Colt ill. Why did they have to put her on the weensy pony and him on this mammoth named after the world's most barfable lunch meat?

But on Liverwurst he was, with a helmet on his head and a wide green nylon belt around his waist and women he didn't know standing one on each side of him, holding him by the belt handles. He was supposed to trust these strangers to keep him from falling off.

Mrs. Berry took his feet and put them in the stirrups. He could tell by looking, not by feeling, that they were in the stirrups. In general, he could not tell where his feet were except by looking. He had no working nerves and muscles in his lower legs and feet, and only a few in his upper legs. Those few let him get around in braces and crutches sometimes, but he found it hard to walk that way. He got tired quickly.

"Ready to ride?" Mrs. Reynolds asked him, standing by Liverwurst's head. She was the one who was supposed to lead the horse. Each handicapped rider had three grown-ups clustered around, one leading and two side-walking.

Colt didn't answer. Why bother? Grown-ups generally did just what they were planning to do anyway. He stared out between Liverwurst's mottled ears, feeling awfully high up. What if he fell . . . yet at the same time he sensed the horse's warm, steady breathing under him. He looked down on shoulders mottled like the sunset in the early-summer sky over the fenced ring where the others were riding.

Why wasn't Liverwurst walking down toward the ring?

"Ready?" Mrs. Reynolds asked again. She was actually waiting for him to say yes.

Colt wondered what would happen if he said no. But in fact, he was sort of ready. He swallowed hard and nodded.

Liverwurst walked.

Colt stiffened and felt his body weight shift an inch to the left. Scared, he strained the reluctant muscles in his right leg and pulled himself back to the center of the saddle before his side walkers could help him. But the next step Liverwurst took pushed him toward the right. He grabbed onto the front of the saddle with both hands.

"Let go, Colt," Mrs. Reynolds instructed over her shoulder. "Relax your back." She stopped the horse and explained to him how he should sit up straight but let himself sway with the gait of the horse.

Liverwurst walked on. Sometimes Colt remembered to loosen his back muscles, sometimes not. It was hard enough for him to make his muscles do what he wanted to anytime, let alone when he was scared, which he was—plenty scared, but still . . . he felt Liverwurst's strong, quiet body moving under him. The thrust of the horse's hind legs and hips surged through Colt, moving his whole body, which actually felt sort of good. Instead of feeling scrunched and heavy and small the way he always did sitting in a wheelchair, Colt felt tall, open, airy, sitting with his feet stretched down toward the earth and his head up toward the sky, high in the saddle. He felt as strong as the deep-breathing horse, and his own chest breathed deep, filled with more than summer air. Filled with the soft clopping of hooves on grass, with rich brown horse-and-leather smells and the way the world looked from up there on a horse's back, up where the breezes were, looking out over people's heads and feeling like—well, like something. Like he really could be a "big guy" who loved horses after all.

Just for a minute he felt that way, and then Liverwurst shook his head to get rid of a fly and Colt grabbed at the saddle, scared all over again.

"We won't let you fall," one side walker, a pudgy woman, told him.

"Do you like riding the horse?" the other woman asked. She spoke slowly and too loudly, as if she thought he was deaf or stupid. A lot of people seemed to think all handicapped kids were retarded. At least Mrs. Berry knew better than that. She always told him he had brains if he would just use them.

He didn't answer the woman but pried his hands loose from the saddle and let them rest on the Appaloosa's mane. He stroked it, trying to get it to lie flat. Warm, coarse hair, lots of colors: black, brown, rust, gold, silver. Liverwurst was as cloudily multicolored as the sunset sky.

"How are you doing, Colt?" Mrs. Berry sang at him the next time she saw him, a few minutes later.

He couldn't admit to her that he was sort of, kind of, enjoying the horse. "My back hurts," he told her, so she had to come over and check his lump and loosen his nylon safety belt.

Chapter Two

Colt's mother and her boyfriend were waiting for him when he finished. (Mrs. Berry had asked Audrey Vittorio not to come for the horseback-riding session itself. Colt tended to "act out" more when his mother was around, Mrs. Berry said.) When Colt saw her waiting for him as he came up to the barn on horseback, he could not help grinning at her. His mother was such a mess ("I am such a mess," she said often and cheerfully) that whenever he saw her he just had to smile.

"Hey! How did it go?" his mother called to him, bouncing like a kid. Her hair, dyed ash-blond instead of being dark like his, was running wild as a mustang. Obviously she had forgotten to comb it again. Her pullover was on backward and inside out, with the tag at her throat like a rectangular jewel. If anyone pointed it out to her, she would giggle with delight. "I'm setting a new style!" she would exclaim.

"How did it go?" Colt's mother insisted eagerly as Mrs. Reynolds stopped Liverwurst near her.

"Okay," Colt admitted. Mrs. Berry was busy with somebody else and wouldn't hear him.

"All *right*! You going to come again next week?"

"Audrey," her boyfriend put in, "later." His name was Brad Flowers, and he had seen Mrs. Berry coming. Colt glanced at him in surprise. It looked as if Brad understood that Colt could not say yes in front of Mrs. Berry, and Colt was not used to that much understanding in an adult, not even in his mother, who was a lot of fun but kind of dense sometimes about what a guy was feeling.

So who the heck was this Brad Flowers that he knew so much? Never having paid much attention to his mother's boyfriends, who had been coming and going since he could remember, Colt had not yet noticed that Brad was different. But now he noticed: Brad had been around longer than any of the others. Six months at least.

Mrs. Berry sailed up. "Ready to get down, Colt?"

"Noooo," he said sarcastically, to annoy her. As usual, it didn't work. She was too busy bossing the two people it took to get him off Liverwurst and into his wheelchair again.

His mother and Brad Flowers had an easier time of it getting him into the backseat of the car. They had more practice, and his mother, who had been lifting him since he was a baby, was big and strong—not chunky, just long limbed, athletic, and deft. Brad Flowers was a husky slow-moving man, raised on a farm before he went into the army. Colt noticed that he didn't drive, the way most of the boyfriends did. Brad let Audrey drive, even though she drove like she talked: awfully fast, with lots of shortcuts.

"Well?" she yelled back at Colt.

"Well, what?"

"You riding again next week?"

"I guess." There was something special about being on top of Liverwurst. A lot better than being under his big rubbery slobbery nose.

"Soon as we get home it'll be time—"

"I *know*."

First thing when he got home Colt had to get to the bathroom and catheterize himself. That is, he had to empty his bladder with a small flexible plastic tube.

Maybe the one thing Colt hated most about spina bifida was that the nerve damage left him without any control of his bodily functions. He always had to be on a schedule to take care of them. He always had to worry about springing a leak and embarrassing himself in public.

Barreling through the living room in his wheelchair on his way to the bathroom, propelling himself over the low-pile carpeting with his hands, Colt nearly ran into a few things: a casserole containing dried-up bits of macaroni and cheese; Muffins, the

Yorkie, eating at the casserole; a cut-glass vase being used as a holder for hammer and screwdrivers while its silk flowers lay dumped to one side; a giant box of Tide on its slow way to the basement; a water-color paint kit laid out to dry, then forgotten; his mother's oxfords in the middle of the floor—she had left her thick white cotton socks draped over the unicorn picture on the wall. (Audrey Vittorio was a postal employee, and Colt often wondered how many pieces of mail she had messed up during any given day.) Also in the living room were Rosie and Lauri Flowers, Brad's kids, looking as out of place as many of the other objects there.

Surprised and a bit flustered to see the Flowers kids, Colt called hi but did not stop to talk. He got himself through the extra-wide bathroom door, found his catheter and sterilizing soap and cotton pads, positioned his wheelchair by the metal stall bars, lifted himself from the wheelchair to the toilet, worked his sweat pants down and took care of himself. Neely was older than he was, and Neely still had his mother or a school nurse do the job. Neely was a wimp. Colt had been catheterizing himself since he was six. It didn't hurt.

He struggled back into his pants, got back into the wheelchair, washed his hands and his catheter, and put everything away. The whole process took a little while, maybe fifteen minutes. Now he would be good for another four hours by the clock. Whoopee.

No hurry. While he was in the bathroom, where

he had some privacy, he did a few of his daily exercises, lifting himself up out of his wheelchair until his arms were straight, then setting himself down again. One, two . . . ten times. Later, once he had cleared a space on his bedroom floor, he would do his sit-ups and push-ups. At least twenty of each. Once, just to show him that he could do it, Mrs. Berry made him do fifty push-ups. He had been sore afterward, but proud, and he had started working out with hand weights too. He had started with a two-pound weight and was working his way up to five. He did not like exercises, but he did them doggedly, day after day, because he knew he had to. Exercises, like catheters, came along with spina bifida.

They were all just sitting in the living room waiting for him when he came out: his mother, and Brad, Rosie, and Lauri. Rosie, despite his name, was a boy, a tall, slim blondish teenager as quiet as his father. Some tease had started calling him "Rosie" because of his last name, Flowers, and the nickname had stuck. He did not seem to mind it. Lauri, his little sister, was about Colt's age, though she looked older. Whenever she was around, Colt watched her with cautious interest.

She was plopped amid the clutter on the floor, looking bored and very pretty. "You're lucky," she complained at Colt as he wheeled his chair up beside her.

"Huh?" He seldom thought of himself as lucky.

"You lucky piece of scum. You got to go horse-back riding."

"Big deal. All they do is put you on the horse and lead it around a ring."

"Hey, I wouldn't mind! How come you get to go horseback riding for free?"

"It's supposed to be good for me."

"No fair! Just because you're handicapped—"

Before Colt could tell her that he'd trade her any-time, her father shushed her. *"Lauri."*

"Want to play something?" Rosie offered Colt vaguely at the same time, trying to smooth things over. They all thought Colt minded Lauri, but he didn't. He liked the way she was honest with him.

"Do *you* want to play something?" he asked her.

She looked annoyed. But before she could answer, her father said, "Don't go off, you guys."

"We want to tell you something," Colt's mother said. Which was not Audrey's usual style at all. Whatever she had to say, she generally just poured it out. And Brad didn't usually even bring his kids to the Vittorio place. Colt had met them maybe twice before, because Rosie and Lauri generally had other things to do besides tag along with their fa-ther. But tonight here they were—and Colt sud-denly noticed how tense and awkward his mother and Brad looked, sitting there on that sofa, just sit-ting.

They looked at each other, each one nudging the other to go first, like a couple of kindergartners coming on stage at a school assembly.

"You tell them," Audrey said, chickening out and passing the buck to Brad.

He tried to joke. "It was your idea."

"Brad, c'mon! You're the guy."

"I'm liberated."

"Tell us *what*?" Colt demanded.

Rosie complained at the same time. "Will one of you just spit it out?"

Flustered, Audrey tried. "Your father—I mean, Brad—well, we—"

"We're going to get married," Brad helped her.

Nobody said congratulations. All three kids looked just plain shocked. Colt gawked at his mother.

"You serious?"

She reached for Brad's hand, and her warm, funny smile was answer enough. But she tried to say more. "Colt, he—he's the one."

Looking back a year or two later, he wondered why he had been so surprised. It was just that, well, there had been other boyfriends. Boyfriends came and went, but Colt stayed. He had kind of thought it would always be just him and her.

Now it was going to be him and her and Brad and . . .

Rosie stood up, moved a few steps closer to his father. "Dad." His voice sounded tight. "Dad, Lauri and I aren't going to have to go back with Mom, are we?"

"Heck, no!" Brad Flowers looked as shocked as his children. "You'll be with me. It's just that we'll be moving here, that's all."

It was going to be Colt and his mother and Brad *and* Rosie *and* Lauri. All in a place not much bigger than a shoe box!

Lauri sat up straight and looked around the chaotic house with a show of alarm.

"I know it's a mess," Audrey apologized, "and I know it's small. But, you see, it has the railings and wide doors and things Colt needs."

Great. Now it's all my *fault.*

"And I can try harder to get myself organized. I've already started clearing the junk out of the spare bedroom—"

Lauri pounced. "Will that be my room?"

"Depends," her father told her. "We have three kids to go into two bedrooms. We figure you can have the one bedroom and Colt and Rosie can share the other. Or you can have the one bedroom and Rosie can sleep on the sofa. Or Rosie can have the spare bedroom and you can sleep on the sofa."

Lauri put up a wail. Rosie looked dazed. Colt burst out, "I don't want somebody else in my room!" Especially not a tall teenage boy like Rosie. Everybody knew (everybody except parents, it seemed) that teenagers were mean and dangerous to younger kids, and that tall boys beat up on smaller boys—held them down by the hair and banged their heads on the ground, even. And Colt would not be able to run away. Who knew what Rosie might do to him in the privacy of a shared bedroom? Rosie might hold him down and twist his arms. Rosie might take away his crutches and braces in the night. Rosie might knock him down and make him break bones and hit his shunt and tear open his lump and *die.*

"I want my room to myself!"

Audrey said, *"Colt—"*

"We don't have to settle it all tonight," Brad put in quietly.

"I don't want to sleep on the sofa!" Lauri wailed.

"Hush up," Mr. Flowers told her, and she hushed. He went on, "Whatever arrangement we come up with, it'll be temporary. Audrey and I are hoping that we'll be able to save enough money by all living together to make a down payment on a bigger house in a year or two."

"A year or two!" Colt yelled. He might be killed by Rosie seventeen times in a year or two.

"COLT!" His mother seldom shouted at him, and even now she didn't look so much angry as ready to cry. "You apologize to Brad!"

"Never mind," Brad said.

And Rosie spoke up in a quiet voice very much like his father's. "Let's just say I'll sleep on the sofa."

Brad told him, "Now, Son, you might not need

to. We have plenty of time, I know we can work this out—"

"It's all right. I'm the oldest. I'll sleep on the sofa." Moving with awkward short steps, Rosie went and stood in front of his father and Audrey Vittorio. "I just want you to be happy," he mumbled, and he leaned over and gave them each a hasty hug.

"Me too," Lauri said, shamefaced. She hurried over to give her dad a long hug. More gingerly she hugged Audrey.

Colt had a miserable feeling that he did not in fact want Brad Flowers and his mother to be happy. He wanted them to be unhappy, so that Brad and his kids would leave and he would have his mother to himself again. Meanwhile, he felt awful, as if he was left out of something important, and it was all his mother's fault.

Keeping his voice very calm, very virtuous, he said to her, "Mom, I can't get over there because of all the junk on the floor."

"Aaaak!" Audrey Vittorio jumped up to clear a path. "I am such a mess."

The next week, when he went to Horseback Riding for the Handicapped, Colt fed Liverwurst a carrot. This was better and less scary than an apple, he found, because he could poke it at Liverwurst while keeping his distance. And Liverwurst did not break it open in so terrifying a way, but merely sucked the long object up into his long mouth, where he chomped it with loud crunching sounds and some orange slobber.

Mrs. Berry made Colt offer the carrot, of course, and Colt fought her all the way. But later, when he was riding Liverwurst with an aide on each side, and Mrs. Reynolds said, "Would you like me to show you how to use the reins?" Colt said, "Yes."

That summer evening he learned to stop the horse with pressure on the reins, to start Liverwurst forward again with a voice command and a tilt of his body, to steer Liverwurst in circles with a signal on the reins and a twist of his head and shoulders, even to ride Liverwurst over a low obstacle. All at a walk, of course. He learned to follow the nodding of the horse's head with his hands, so that the bit at the other end of the taut reins would not hurt Liverwurst's mouth. He even managed once to nudge Liverwurst into a walk with his legs.

"Wonderful, Colt!" Mrs. Berry beamed at him. "Excellent posture!"

He was sitting up straight because it felt good and because it helped him ride the horse properly, not because she said so. She should know that. The horse took cues from the position of his body, Mrs. Reynolds had explained, as well as from the reins. Didn't Mrs. Berry understand these things? Her compliment annoyed him because good posture was not the point, at least not to him. Riding the horse was.

Riding the horse was really something.

24 ·

·COLT·

His mother and Brad were waiting for him after the hour of horseback riding was over. He ignored them as Mrs. Berry pushed him in his wheelchair up the lumpy driveway to them, looking instead over his shoulder at the horse being led into the barn.

So his mother was getting married to this guy he barely knew. So he was going to have three strangers living in his house, all of them healthy and stronger than he. So he was a poor wimp of a handicapped kid in a wheelchair. So what. At least there was one thing in his life—a big, powerful thing—he could control.

"See ya later, Liverwurst," he called.

Chapter Three

"Are there bears?" Colt demanded.

"Not likely," Mrs. Reynolds answered him, in her usual level way. She was walking along beside him as one of his aides. Colt no longer needed anyone at Liverwurst's head. He took care of guiding and controlling the horse these days. He could make Liverwurst walk on, stop, back up, do circles and serpentines and figure eights, go over a low jump, and run relay races. Or walk relay races, rather. So far all the handicapped kids were riding just at a walk.

The next week, Mrs. Reynolds had just told him, he was going to get to ride Liverwurst outside the ring. The handicapped class was going out on the trails in the wooded state park nearby.

"But there are *some* bears," Colt insisted. He was

scared of large wild animals. "There are bears in the woods in Pennsylvania. People hunt them."

"That's up in the mountains, mostly," Mrs. Reynolds told him.

"Some of them could come down here. What'll happen if we run into a bear?"

Almost offhand Mrs. Reynolds said, "If Liverwurst even so much as smelled a bear he would rear up and throw you off and run home like a racehorse."

Oddly, this blunt statement of truth made Colt feel much better than any assurance could have. He said, "You're not worried?"

"I've been riding around here for twenty years and never run into a bear yet."

"But there *could* be bears."

"Probably not. You have to think in terms of probabilities, Colt."

"Huh?" Mrs. Reynolds always talked to him as if he were her equal, and he liked that. But sometimes he had to ask her to repeat or explain. Like now. "Think in terms of what?"

"Probabilities," she told him. "Nothing's ever absolutely safe or certain. You have to go with what's probably going to happen. It's like that when you're dealing with horses, and it's like that when you're dealing with life."

He guided Liverwurst into a circle, swiveling his shoulders and hips toward the direction he wanted the horse to go, hinting with the reins and squeezing as much as he could (which wasn't much) with the leg toward the center of the circle. Liverwurst turned his neck in an arc that matched the line Colt wanted and clopped on.

"So there's probably no bears out there," Colt said to Mrs. Reynolds.

"The chances are very, very small that we will meet a bear."

He considered, then offered a small joke. "What about mountain lions?"

She laughed. "*Right*, Colt."

But part of him really was worrying about mountain lions. Even though he knew it made no sense, he couldn't seem to help being scared of things.

He worried about bears, and sometimes mountain lions, off and on throughout the next week. Not too much, because he had plenty of other things to worry about. The bad grades he was getting in his summer tutoring, for one. His mother always had him tutored over the summer, because the way fluid buildup had affected his central nervous system made him have trouble with schoolwork, especially with math. And when he got bad grades in the summer she really got mad, because she was paying the tutor.

And the wedding, for another thing. He worried that he would stumble going up the carpeted aisle, when everybody would be looking at him. Or a crutch would slip. Or he would get too tired, standing in his braces. He was supposed to be up front with his mother and hand her the ring she was going to put on Brad, and he worried that he would drop it. It wasn't going to be a big fancy wedding, but still he worried that he would embarrass himself somehow.

He worried about the wedding on the way to the stable the next week, and then getting ready for the trail ride he started to worry about large wild animals. But meanwhile he felt quite glad to see a certain large tame animal.

"Hi, Liverwurst!" he greeted the horse when an aide wheeled him into the stable. "Hey, boy!" The horse stuck his splotchy head out over the stall door, and Colt reached up and patted him, rubbing hard at the itchy place just under Liverwurst's forelock. Liverwurst thrust his head down as far as he could get it, his big rubbery nose almost against Colt's chest and the good horse smell of him strong in Colt's face. Colt fed him his apple. It no longer bothered him that Liverwurst chomped and slobbered. Colt chomped and slobbered himself sometimes, especially when he was faced with spaghetti, and he guessed there were some people who thought he was ugly because he had a shunt in his head and the top part of him was big compared to the bottom. But Liverwurst no longer looked ugly to Colt.

Mrs. Reynolds came in with that long, strong, blue-jeaned stride of hers. "Ready to ride, Colt?"

"I guess."

He worried about finishing his homework while the volunteers got him on his horse, and he worried about the wedding while he picked up the reins, and he worried about bears and wolves and mountain lions as he rode Liverwurst up the farm lane and along a country road to the state forest. And then he was on the trail, and somehow (he never quite understood how it happened) he wasn't scared and he wasn't worrying about anything.

Out there the whole world was made of tall pines and green light and spicy-sweet air and the long, tan, wandering trail. And it was all shining new. Colt had never been in such a place before because crutches or a wheelchair would not take him there, but now he was part of it. Hushed shade, the soft clop of hooves, the rhythm of the walk, his own body, swaying, swaying—he no longer felt separate from these things, no longer felt somehow outside of his life looking in. He just—was. Liverwurst was Liverwurst, and Colt was Colt.

Behind him he could hear cutesy-pie little Julie giggling on her pony. Jay Gee and Neely were singing off-key somewhere up ahead, and the women on each side of him were conversing about Mexican food, and it was all good, all part of tall green shade and hoof clop, and Colt's life felt big enough to include it all. Big as forest and cool pine sky.

And lake. There was a lake up ahead.

The trail dipped down toward it, and there was no need to worry, no need even to think, just shift

weight in the saddle and give Liverwurst a little more
rein and let him manage the slope, nodding all the
while as if he understood. Colt noticed without fear
that his side walkers no longer bothered to hold on
to the handles of his safety belt. When the trail nar-
rowed and grew even steeper the women dropped
behind, first one and then the other, while the aides
who had to stay beside their handicapped riders
struggled through brush and poison ivy.

I'm riding on my own. . . .

And he was looking down a sheer drop into deep
water on one side, and on the other side he was
looking up a steep hillside pierced with pines so tall
they seemed to topple, they would all fall into the
lake—he would fall. But even as he thought it,
somehow he knew he would not. He and Liverwurst could manage this situation. Something warm
and strong and vital seemed to flow up to him out
of his horse, maybe out of the earth itself through
the horse's solid striding hooves.

Right down to his bones Colt knew two things:

I am alive.

I am a horseback rider.

The trail climbed the sheer lakeside slope to the
hilltop, where there was a clearing. Mrs. Reynolds
and one of the helpers set Colt down on the ground,
where he ate watermelon as messily as Liverwurst
had ever eaten anything (and fed the rind to his
horse), and Mrs. Berry made a speech thanking Mrs.
Reynolds for the use of Deep Meadows Farm and

her horses and ponies. It was July, time for the volunteers to go off on their vacations. It was the last day of the summer's horseback riding program.

Back on Liverwurst again, holding the reins with sticky hands, going home, even with the daylight fading under the dark pines Colt still did not feel afraid. Not of horses or wildcats or the wedding. Not of anything.

The feeling lasted clear through his night's sleep and through the next day until the wedding rehearsal.

Colt did not particularly embarrass himself or anyone else at the wedding. He wore protection so that he would not have to worry about his wayward personal functions. He did not stumble as he walked up the aisle with his mother (noticing that getting around on crutches did not seem as tiring as it used to) and stood beside her with his braces rumpling his one good suit. Standing, he used his left crutch only, slipping his hand out of the cuff of the right one so that he could hand her the ring when it was time. He noticed how pretty she looked. He noticed that he himself felt fine. He did not drop the ring. True, when he lifted his hand to give it to his mother, his right crutch clattered to the floor, but nobody giggled. Brad wasn't bothered; he just looked over and smiled at Colt. It took a lot, apparently, to upset Brad. Even getting married to Audrey Vittorio didn't seem to bother him too much. Lauri, who was holding Audrey's flowers, gave Colt a scornful look as she picked up the crutch and handed it back to him, but girls always looked scornful, Colt had found. And Rosie, who was Brad's best man, did not seem to notice anything. There was a sort of patient anxious-eyed Liverwurst look about Rosie.

Colt kept on feeling fine right through the reception. And when he had a chance, when people weren't talking to him, he sat and thought.

He dreamed, rather. Of things he had seen at Deep Meadows Farm. Of horses sailing up fields at a long-reaching trot. Of horses cantering, their manes floating like wings. Of riders flying along on top of the trot and rocking to the rhythm of the canter. Of the trail, of the deep-green distances under the pine trees. Of freedom. Of going far. Of riding—not just poking around a ring at a walk, but really riding . . .

He had to talk with his mother. He waited as long as he could, which was until the day after the wedding, when Brad and Rosie and Lauri moved in.

"Mom. There's something I really want."

She looked up at him from the living-room floor, where she was struggling to clear a space around the sofa for Rosie. The problem was the two months worth of newspapers and magazines piled under and around what was to be Rosie's bed. Audrey looked hassled. At least she had had her dinner. Colt had made himself wait until past the height of the commotion and after dinner.

"Mom, I want to keep on horseback riding."

She nodded without very much comprehension. "They'll have handicapped riding again next summer."

"No!" Colt made himself lower his voice. This was serious, not something he wanted to get his mother angry about. "I don't mean next summer with the other Easter Seals kids. I mean now, the rest of this summer."

Audrey blinked. "You mean paid private lessons? With Mrs. Reynolds?"

"Yeah. Something like that." Colt wasn't too clear on the details. He just knew he had to get on Liverwurst again and learn how to go faster. Trot. Maybe even canter.

His mother turned back to her excavations. "I don't know, hon. I've got a lot on me right now. You remember we're supposed to be saving money for a house—"

"Mom, *please*. It's important."

She looked at him again, thinking, and her hesitation told him she wanted to say yes. But she said, "It's not just me you want to talk with anymore. You've got to include Brad."

It was a couple of days before Colt could work himself up to do that. Which was just as well, because the household was in chaos. Audrey worked eight to five at the post office, but Brad was working three to eleven at the munitions plant, and Lauri had to be up at four in the morning to deliver her paper route. Since the route was back in the neighborhood where the Flowerses used to live, Audrey or her dad had to drive her. Rosie, who worked until past midnight at the McDonald's, was always on the sofa trying to sleep when Lauri and Audrey or Brad came through the living room on their way out the door, at which point Muffins, who considered all the newcomers dangerous intruders, always sounded the alarm. Daytimes were not much better. Lauri had gymnastics and swimming and viola lessons, Colt had tutoring, Rosie had to go jogging to prepare for the cross-country season, Brad was trying to sleep, and Muffins barked at everything that moved. There were boxes and piles of Flowers junk all over the floors, nobody was getting enough sleep, and nobody ever knew who was supposed to cook what, or for how many, or when.

Colt could not wait until after it sorted out to make his next horseback-riding request. Over the weekend, when Brad and his mother were both home at once, he got them to sit on the sofa (on top of Rosie's sleeping bag) and listen to him. This time he had done some preparation.

"I called Mrs. Reynolds," he said, "and she said yes, she could give me private lessons on Liverwurst if Mrs. Berry thought it was a good idea. So I called Mrs. Berry, and she thinks it's a great idea. She says I'm sitting up straighter and my back is stronger and my balance is better since I did that little bit of horseback riding." Consciously he sat straight, not touching the back of the soft living-room chair he was perched in. He had been making a silent point of not spending so much time in his wheelchair, and was using his crutches and leg braces more than he used to. The crutches sat in the chair beside him.

Brad nodded. Audrey said, "I've noticed it too, that you're looking stronger."

Colt said, "So Mrs. Reynolds says fine with her as long as it's okay with you." He brought forth what he considered his strongest point. "And since I'm one of the handicapped kids she'll only charge us half price for the lessons."

Brad looked amazed. "Actually, she could charge us double," he said.

"People can be incredibly nice," Audrey told him. "I never get surprised anymore at how generous people can be."

Colt jiggled, waiting impatiently for the answer he wanted. "So can I call her and tell her it's okay?"

His mother was ready to say yes, he could tell. But Brad said, "Hold on a minute."

Colt hated him. He tried not to show it, but his voice sounded hard and snide as he said, "If it's the money, I can stop getting my allowance—"

"It's not the money," Brad said. "If we can afford three kinds of lessons for Lauri, we can afford horseback riding lessons for you. What worries me is the risk."

Audrey looked at him in surprise. "It didn't look

to me as if those horses would ever do anything to hurt anyone."

Brad touched her knee but didn't answer. Instead, he looked straight at Colt. "What do you have in mind? Just walking around in the ring?"

Brad understood too much, darn him. Colt didn't know how he understood so well, but something in his level gaze told Colt he did, and Colt knew there was no use trying to fool him. He decided to start his risk-taking right away. He took a deep breath and said, "I want to learn to really ride, not just plod along with a bunch of baby-sitters. I want to go out on the trails. I want to go faster than a walk. I want to . . ." He let his voice trickle away, not sure how to say what riding meant to him.

But Brad seemed to know. He nodded. "See, I used to ride horses when I was a kid," he said. "Rode when I was in the service too." He looked at Audrey. "People who work around horses, like Mrs. Reynolds, they get used to the danger, they don't think about it. And Mrs. Berry, I don't think she's ever been on a horse. She wouldn't know what might happen." Brad went on quickly, quietly. "Even on the safest horse, there's always a chance it might spook or bolt, if something scares it bad enough. And even the best riders take falls. Horseback riding's risky."

Colt felt his hands quivering, he was so angry at Brad. So furious he couldn't speak, not even to yell or bawl or throw a fit, because his mother, who would have said yes if it was just her decision, was looking at Brad with wide eyes. "Then you don't think Colt should do it?"

"I didn't say that. I just want you to know. It's you I'm worried about, mostly. He's your kid. You've got to understand that he could get hurt or even killed."

Colt said, his voice shaking, "I could spend my life never doing anything important to me, and I could still get hurt."

"I know that." Brad looked back at him, and when their eyes met all Colt's anger swirled away like water down a drain. He felt weak, and was glad he was sitting down. There was something better than pity in Brad's eyes. Better even than compassion. He began to understand why his mother had married Brad.

Audrey said quietly, "Let me see if I've got it straight. On the one hand horseback riding will help Colt's strength and balance—"

"It'll help more than that," Brad said.

"But on the other hand it's more dangerous than I had thought."

"It's not like it's skydiving or something. But it is risky."

Colt said, his voice steady this time, "Mrs. Reynolds said nothing's ever certain. She said I ought to think in terms of probabilities. Like, I probably

·COLT·

won't ever get hurt on Liverwurst because he's a
real calm horse."

Audrey nodded at him, and said to Brad, "What
do you think?"

"It's up to you."

She said, "He's growing up. I think he's got to try
new things. Take a few chances."

Brad said, "I think so too."

Colt did not yell yahoo or move or smile. It was
a serious moment.

His mother said to him, "You are to keep me in-
formed of everything you do with the horse."

He nodded.

"You are always to have someone with you. You
are not to ride alone."

He nodded. It was a promise. "You'll call Mrs.
Reynolds and set a time?"

"On one condition." But now there was mischief
in his mother's eyes, and satisfaction, because she
had him where she wanted him and was going to
get her way about something. "Rosie is going to
share your room. And that is that. Do we understand each other, young man?"

Colt nodded.

Chapter Four

Trundling around his room belly-down on his scooter board, rearranging his stuff to make room for Rosie, Colt indulged in peevish thoughts. Why couldn't things be simple? Take the scooter board, for instance. It looked simple, a lot like a skateboard meant for him to lie on as he pushed himself along with his hands. Fine, great, no wheelchair, no crutches and braces. But no good way to carry things either. He had to tuck stuff under his chin. And then when he got to the other side of the room he couldn't reach any high places. If he used his wheelchair instead of the scooter board he couldn't reach any low places. No matter how he tried to do it, changing his room around was a pain. And it was all Rosie's fault—for being born.

Colt considered that he was not yet defeated regarding that large, healthy intruder of a teenager.

He had heard that sometimes the best defense was a good offense. And he knew he was good at being offensive. Maybe he could annoy Rosie enough so that he would voluntarily move out again. At the very least he could save his own pride. He could short-sheet Rosie's bed before Rosie got a chance to short-sheet his. Short-sheeting was the least of what he could do to Rosie.

Of course, he had to cover his own rear. His mother might take away his horseback-riding lessons if Rosie complained. But if he did things Rosie would be embarrassed to tell about, then his mother would never know.

Colt sat up on his scooter board and watched as his mother and Brad brought in a studio couch and set it along the far wall from his bed. He watched as they put sheets and a lightweight summer blanket on it (flowered sheets—his mother didn't own any other kind). After they had gone off to the kitchen, Colt made a quiet trip to the bathroom, then pulled back Rosie's top sheet and sprinkled Rosie's bed and pillow thickly with the potent rose-scented talcum powder his great-aunt Letitia, who sold Avon, had given his mother for Christmas. He smoothed down the top sheet again and returned the powder to its place.

Because he was in training for cross-country running, Rosie was supposed to go to bed early when he could. (This had been quite a problem when he was sleeping on the sofa.) So, as Rosie had the day off from McDonald's, Colt was able to enjoy the show that evening as Rosie got into his new bed, laid his head on his pillow with a grateful sigh, and then made a strangled noise. Colt lay grinning in his own bed, and when Rosie sat up and gave him a look, he just kept grinning. Rosie didn't say anything. He swung his long, muscular, very hairy legs out of the sheets, pulled the blanket up, took the pillowcase off the pillow and dropped it to the floor, where it settled with a white puff of talc. Then he lay down on top of the blanket, turned off the light, and went to sleep.

"Rosie," Colt's mother asked her stepson in puzzled tones a few days later, "why are you sleeping on top of your bed instead of in it? Is something wrong?"

"Nah. I just feel like it."

Meanwhile, Colt had dropped Rosie's jockstrap down behind the dresser, spilled Kool-Aid in his running shoes ("Oops! Sorry, Rosie"), and slimed the doorknob with shaving cream so that Rosie, who always got up around three in the morning to go to the bathroom, would find it in the dark with his groggy hand. (He got a satisfying squeak out of Rosie on that occasion.) He also left a few surprise snacks, such as Jell-O, on Rosie's bed for him to find when he came home late from work.

Nothing happened in response to all this except that Rosie took to turning on the light whenever he needed to move around the room at night.

·COLT·

Evidently Rosie was not the sort to tattle. Colt was enjoying himself, but at the same time starting to feel desperate. Rosie hadn't done anything mean to him. Rosie seemed to have patience that would put Mrs. Berry to shame.

What do I have to do to get a reaction out of this guy?

It was the sight of Rosie's athletic and darkly furred legs stretched naked in the summertime heat on top of his talcum-tainted bed that gave Colt his best idea yet.

His excitement helped him stay awake. After Rosie was asleep (and Colt knew by then that Rosie was a sound sleeper), Colt started to move.

Down off his bed—headfirst, balancing on his arms, as always. He did not want to use his scooter board, which was too noisy, despite Rosie's sleeping abilities, so he combat-crawled. All the push-ups had made his arms and shoulders strong enough to drag the rest of him along. It took a while, but he got himself to the bathroom and found what he wanted. In fact, he had located it earlier in the day and moved it to the cabinet under the sink, where he could reach it easily—his mother's "Fast-Action Foam Hair Remover." And a supply of damp sponges, of course.

He had read the instructions and thought ahead, premoistening the sponges and storing them in a plastic bag. Everything he needed was waiting for him.

When he got back to the bedroom with the stuff, Colt pulled himself to his knees at the side of Rosie's bed, pointed the hair-remover nozzle downward, and squirted the stinky foam on his stepbrother's bare legs, from his briefs right on down to his ankles.

The streetlamps outside gave him enough light to work by. Using his fingers lightly, carefully, he spread the foam so that it covered the back half of Rosie's legs. Rosie happened to be lying on his stomach. It did not bother Colt that he and the hair remover could not reach the thick growth on Rosie's shins and the fronts of Rosie's thighs. In Colt's opinion, the two-tone effect would be stunning.

He gave the foam the few minutes it needed to do its job, then removed it (along with Rosie's leg hair) with his damp sponges.

He had finished one leg to his complete satisfaction and was halfway through the other before Rosie woke up, grunted a wordless inquiry, and reared up on his hands, swiveling to look.

"Lie still," Colt ordered him cheerfully. "I'm almost done."

Rosie did in fact hold still for a moment longer, too startled to react. But then, with a yell of despair—the throaty bellow of a person pushed past his limits—he lashed around and lunged at his tormenter. Colt froze, terrified, realizing too late that if Rosie knocked him down, if he landed on his back and hit his lump . . .

·COLT·

This is it. I've gone too far. I'm gonna die.

But Rosie stopped just short of him, hands shaking in the air.

"You!" Rosie screamed. "You—" And then Rosie choked back the words.

"Go ahead!" All of Colt's terror suddenly left him, and instead he felt deeply excited, earnest, sincere. He was an experimenter on the verge of a breakthrough. "Say it! What were you about to say?"

Rosie grabbed the sponges dripping on his bed and threw them across the room.

"Say it!" Colt begged. "Please!" Rosie had been about to call him names, and he very much wanted to hear them.

Rosie glowered. "Can't," he muttered.

"Why *not?*"

"Because Dad told me—" Breathing heavily, wiping gunk off his ankle with the one remaining sponge, Rosie panted out the words. "Because— Dad—told me to try to get along with you, no matter how much of a brat you were."

"Really?" Colt was so delighted his voice squeaked. "Your dad said I was a brat?"

Rosie stared at him.

"Did he really say I was a brat?" Colt insisted. "I mean, that's the word he used and everything?"

No longer angry, Rosie looked less like a madman and more like Liverwurst: wide-eyed, bewildered. "Why the heck," Rosie pleaded, "do you want people to call you a brat?"

"Because . . ." Colt could not explain how being a brat made him real. How most people, looking at him, saw only the handicap, the braces and crutches, the wheelchair, and felt they had to be nice to him no matter what. Therefore, he had to make them *not* be nice to him. No matter what. "Just tell me what your father called me," he said.

"What kind of trouble are you getting me into?"

"Oh, okay." Colt saw Rosie's point of view. For a moment he slumped against Rosie's bed, discouraged, but then his head came up. "Do *you* think I'm a brat?" he demanded.

Rosie looked straight at him. "You are an incredible brat."

It was a moment too good for smiles. Rosie understood. Rosie saw past the crutches to Colt.

"You might be the top brat of all time." Rosie stood up to examine his legs. Even in the dim bedroom light the half-shaved effect was startling. "Aw, maaan," Rosie lamented. "Aw, CRUD! What the heck am I gonna do? I can't wear pants and run."

The room light flicked on, making Colt and Rosie cower a moment in its glare. At the door stood Brad and Audrey Flowers, roused by Rosie's yelling. They did not seem totally sleepy. Apparently they had been listening for a few minutes. So it was no use trying to pretend nothing was happening, and anyway the room reeked of hair remover, and Rosie was standing there with two-tone legs.

Brad looked blank. Colt's mother looked horrified. "Colt Vittorio," she burst out with tears in her voice, "how could you?"

It occurred to Colt that he was the only one in the house whose last name was not Flowers. He felt left out of something good, and guilty that he had upset his mother. He didn't mind making her mad, but he hated to hurt her. "Sorry, Mom," he mumbled.

"If this is the way you're going to act—"

Brad's quiet voice interrupted her. "Well, Son," he said to Rosie, deadpan, eyeing Rosie's legs, "you look like a '56 DeSoto."

Father and son looked at each other, and a smile cracked Mr. Flowers's poker face, and suddenly Rosie was laughing, guffawing, shouting with laughter, bent over with his hands on his knees. Brad chuckled more quietly. "This is a night Rosie is going to remember," he said to Audrey.

But she was not done with Colt. "I don't understand what gets into you," she scolded. "Maybe I ought to tell you to just forget about horseback riding until next summer."

"No!" Rosie straightened suddenly, his face shocked and serious. "Audrey, I mean Mom, this was just something between me and Colt. He didn't mean anything. Please."

Colt was so startled to find someone else doing his pleading for him that for a moment he couldn't speak. Then in a small voice he said, "I won't hassle Rosie anymore."

It was the truth. Rosie was a friend after all, like Liverwurst. Colt felt glad he hadn't put the hair remover anyplace serious, like Rosie's head.

"It's just boy stuff, hon," Brad said to his wife.

Still more hurt and baffled than angry, Audrey grumbled, "Well, I don't know . . ."

"He won't do anything else to me," Rosie said as if promising for Colt. "Because he knows if he does, I'll do it right back to him. No more Mr. Nice Guy. Right, brat?" Rosie grinned at Colt. Past him Colt could see Brad's laughing eyes. These Flowers guys had something good between them, and they were offering to include him in it.

"Right!" said Colt.

When practice started, the last week of July, Rosie told his cross-country teammates that he had gotten himself a special aerodynamic leg clip originated by the Olympic running coach. To smiling passersby as he jogged he muttered something about racing stripes. To his sister he said that he would punch her lights out if he heard one more word. To Colt and his father he maintained that the hair remover treatment really seemed to be helping him run faster. His time had mysteriously improved over the previous year's.

All that hair, his father gravely agreed, had been slowing him down. Maybe he ought to defuzz his legs regularly, as he did his face.

·COLT·

On that basis, Audrey remarked, a shaved race-horse should run faster.

And Colt sat in his thigh-high leg braces and dreamed of going fast, faster, on a horse.

His riding lessons had started. ("You scum!" Lauri had complained, and she had called her father at work to see if she could get him to promise her horseback riding lessons the next summer instead of gymnastics.) Because of the summertime heat, lessons took place in the evening, which worked out for Colt's mother. By that time of day she was home from work and could take Colt to Deep Meadows Farm.

For the first few weeks Lauri came along too, and watched wistfully. After that she quit coming. It just made her mad, she said.

Mrs. Reynolds had arranged for Colt to have his lessons by himself, because she wanted to give him her full attention. He wore a helmet and safety belt borrowed from Mrs. Berry. After Mrs. Reynolds found that he could consistently keep his balance on a walking horse, she stopped staying right by his side. Leaning against the ring's rail fence, she called instructions to him, watching him guide Liverwurst in circles and reverses and along diagonals.

"You have good hands," she told him. "You keep a nice, steady, light contact with the mouth. I like to see that. I hate to see a rider dragging on the horse's mouth."

Colt said, "I try to think what it would feel like if I were the horse."

"We'll make a horseman of you yet."

After a few weeks she put him into a class of non-handicapped beginning riders. Colt could do everything the others could do at a walk, but while they practiced posting to a trot he halted Liverwurst in the center of the ring, doing saddle exercises and watching. The trot was a piston-action two-beat gait, bumping the riders along until they learned to rise and sink, rise and sink in the saddle. When Mrs. Reynolds demonstrated, posting to the rhythm of her own thoroughbred's long, reaching trot, she seemed to skim the world like a meadowlark.

Colt's mother, who was sitting on a bench reading a paperback novel while he had his lesson, lifted her eyes from time to time and watched him anxiously. He wished she wouldn't stick around while he rode, but she always did. She had to help Mrs. Reynolds get him onto Liverwurst and off again, and she said by the time she went anywhere else it would be time to come back again. But if she was going to stay, he wished she would pay more attention to her book.

He decided what he wanted to say to her, then waited until after the other riders had gone, until he had her alone, except for Mrs. Reynolds. Actually, he spoke to Janet Reynolds, although he wanted his mother to hear. "Mrs. Reynolds," he said softly, "I want to learn how to trot. Maybe even canter. I want to go fast on a horse. And I want to go out on the trails."

Wanna, wanna, wanna. It could have sounded bratty, but it did not. Even Colt noticed it did not. Funny how he never got bratty when he was talking about horseback riding.

Mrs. Reynolds looked back at him just as seriously.

"Can he do those things?" Colt's mother asked her. "I mean is it possible?"

"I don't know," she replied to both of them. She knew Colt could raise himself from the saddle for short periods of time. Maybe he would be able to post to a trot. But whether his seat would ever be tight enough for safety at a canter . . . "I don't know. We'll just have to work, and see."

Chapter Five

Colt worked.

He had just enough strength in his upper legs to kneel. Sometimes. Every day at home he practiced to strengthen his posting muscles by kneeling without support. Mrs. Reynolds had said that he needed strength in his abdominal muscles to post too, so he did sit-ups as well. Or rather, more sit-ups than usual. And, while he was at it, push-ups.

Rosie had exercises to do too, for cross-country, warm-ups and stretches. He would sprawl on the bedroom floor and limber his legs. One day, feeling companionable, Colt joined him and started doing push-ups.

Rosie stared a moment, then flipped over on his belly and started doing push-ups too.

Cold did more push-ups.

Rosie did more push-ups.

·COLT·

Colt speeded the tempo a bit, doing push-ups faster.

Rosie matched his roommate's pace and started to pant.

Colt began counting aloud. "Forty, forty-one . . . How many you want to do, Rosie?"

"As—many—as—you're good for," Rosie puffed.

"Okay." Cheerfully Colt pumped his way to fifty. Fifty push-ups was no big deal to him any longer.

Past fifty, he noticed, Rosie slowed down a good bit. Colt slowed down to stay with him, and counted his way aloud through the sixties. He had just hit seventy and was aiming for seventy-five when Rosie collapsed on the floor with a groan.

"God! How can you *do* that?"

"Do—what?" Colt was puffing now too, but still pumping. He figured since he was feeling good he'd try for a hundred push-ups.

"All those push-ups, turkey!"

"Don't worry—it's not your fault." Breathing hard, Colt still managed to insult Rosie between efforts. "Everybody knows—cross-country runners are no good—at push-ups."

"Aw, jeez! You better watch out. I'm gonna sneak in here some night and take all the hair off your arms."

Colt grinned and quit at eighty-five.

Someday he'd get to a hundred. He might need strong arms someday, to control a headstrong horse. But for now he mostly needed posting muscles. Once he could kneel steadily, he tried to lower himself backward a little as if to sit down, then come up again. He held imaginary reins in front of his chest so that he would not use his hands to help himself.

I—can't—do it.

Tried again.

I—gotta—do it!

He couldn't, at first. And then after a few days he could do it once, just barely, maybe an inch. And then after a couple of weeks of hard work he could do it a few times, maybe two inches deep. Lauri tried it with him sometimes, and she could sit on her feet and come back up again without using her hands. But Lauri was a gymnast. And Lauri did not have spina bifida.

Altogether Colt was working his body harder than he ever had in his life, and Mrs. Berry, who saw him twice a week for physical therapy, was amazed at the results.

"His large-muscle strength in his torso has improved so much I can't *believe* it," she reported to his mother. "He's sitting better, standing better, his endurance is a *lot* better, his balance is better, his walking gait has improved. I'm really hoping someday he'll give up the wheelchair except for shopping malls and such, and just use his braces and crutches most of the time."

During his weekly lessons at Deep Meadows Farm, Colt practiced staying up off the saddle in "forward position" for as long as he could, at first with Mrs.

Reynolds's help and later by himself. There were problems. Because Colt had no strength or feeling below his knees, he could not rely on his stirrups to support him. Sometimes his feet dangled out of the stirrups and he didn't even know it. He had to maintain his riding seat entirely with his upper body and thighs. This, Mrs. Reynolds assured him, was as it should be in any event. Judges at horse shows often asked advanced contestants to ride without their stirrups to show that they were not dependent on them. The lower leg was needed mostly to urge on and signal the horse. But Colt could use his body position and reins for signaling, and a stick for urging on.

Liverwurst stood or walked patiently through all this. Good old big-headed Liverwurst. Colt had come to love the horse's homely, anxious, hairy, snot-nosed face.

Finally, one evening in late August, just before school was due to start, Mrs. Reynolds came over to Colt, took hold of his safety belt and said, "Okay, let's try a trot."

Okay, sports fans, this is it, the moment you've been waiting for . . . Even though he tried to joke with himself, Colt felt so nervous his head throbbed.

The hardest thing, Mrs. Reynolds told him, was going to be learning to feel the rhythm and post to it. Because of his back, she couldn't let him just bounce around on top of the horse for a while as she did the others. She had put a fleece cover on the saddle for him, but even so, it would not be a good idea for him to bounce.

"Stay up in forward position for now," she told him, and she stood beside him, her arm between him and the saddle, just in case. "This time I'll let you cheat and use a voice command."

"Trot!" Colt told Liverwurst.

The horse could not believe him. It had all been walk, walk, walk with Colt up until now. Liverwurst raised his head anxiously but did not move.

"Try again, and tap him with the crop," said Mrs. Reynolds.

"Trot!"

Liverwurst trotted. It was just a quiet jog, but to Colt it felt like one of the delightful, scary amusement park rides he had never been allowed on. His stomach fluttered, his shoulders tingled, and he had to concentrate on staying up out of the saddle. His knees acted as shock absorbers, and his bottom waggled in the air. Mrs. Reynolds ran alongside, keeping her arm between him and the saddle.

"Neat!" Colt panted happily. His breath was being jounced out of him. From her seat outside the ring, his mother lifted her glance from her paperback romance and watched anxiously.

"Liverwurst has a pretty smooth trot," puffed Mrs. Reynolds. "For an Appaloosa. Had enough?"

"No."

She had him stop Liverwurst anyway, because *she*

had had enough. But after she caught her breath,
they tried it again.

"Now this time try to signal with your knees for
the trot."

A normal rider would have squeezed with the
lower leg. But it didn't matter: Liverwurst, having
learned that he was allowed to trot, jogged forward
happily at the light pressure Colt was able to exert
on him.

"Try to feel the rhythm! Go up and down! ONE-
two-ONE-two . . ."

It was not easy. Several times Colt bumped down
into Mrs. Reynolds's arm. Then she ran out of breath
again and had to stop. By the end of the lesson all
she would say was, "We'll see. Things take time."

Colt's mother was quiet for a change as she drove
him home.

The next week school began, and Colt's riding lesson time changed. He came late Saturday afternoon.

"Hey, Liverwurst!" He rubbed the horse's mottled forehead. Liverwurst thrust his nose down and
nuzzled Colt's chest. Then it was time to roll the
wheelchair up the ramp and get onto the horse. Mrs.
Reynolds and Colt had come up with a way he could
mount with only one person to help him. He could
get on his knees at the edge of the ramp and reach
up to grasp Liverwurst's withers and the saddle can-

tle, just the way regular riders did. Then Mrs. Reynolds would give him a "leg up" the way she sometimes did with anyone trying to mount a tall horse. She would cradle both hands under his left knee and lift while he pulled with his arms, and as she lifted, he could swing himself into the saddle. (His right foot dragged across Liverwurst's rump, but Liverwurst didn't mind.) This was all Colt's idea. In a few years, he knew, he would be too big and heavy to be lifted onto a horse, and he wanted always to be able to ride. He didn't want anything, ever, to keep him from riding horseback.

Colt's mother went and took her seat on her bench. Even though she no longer had to help him get on the horse, Audrey stayed to watch his lessons anyway, pretending to read.

"Okay," Mrs. Reynolds said once Colt was settled on top of Liverwurst and had gathered up his reins, "take him on down to the ring."

Colt had done this a dozen times, maybe more. He turned Liverwurst toward the ring and gave him a gentle squeeze with his knees to tell him to walk.

Liverwurst snorted happily and jumped forward into a brisk trot.

Colt had never in his life been bounced, not even on a grandparent's knee, and the shock of what he was feeling stunned him so badly that he couldn't react. Every functioning muscle in his body stiffened in protest. He heard Mrs. Reynolds shouting, "Pull on the reins! Make him whoa!" But her voice sounded as if it were coming through ten feet of water, and he could not do what she said—he had lost the reins. He tried to get in forward position, but his knees weren't tight. He was hanging on by the mane and felt himself slipping farther sideways at every jounce. He was going to fall off! And he felt hurt to the heart. *Liverwurst, how can you do this to me?* Colt had thought the horse was his friend. Tears blinded him so that he couldn't even see, and, dammit, he hated crying. . . .

The horrible jouncing stopped, Liverwurst stopped trotting and stood still so suddenly that Colt almost pitched forward over his neck. But his hands caught him. He straightened and started automatically fumbling for the reins. He blinked away tears and found that he had come perhaps thirty feet from the mounting ramp, only halfway to the ring. Mrs. Reynolds was running up beside him. His mother stood in front of him, holding Liverwurst by the bridle. Audrey Flowers, who had never handled a horse in her life, had jumped out in front of Liverwurst and made him stop trotting.

"I'm so sorry!" Mrs. Reynolds panted, taking hold of Liverwurst's bridle from the other side. "He must have got it in his head last time that he's supposed to trot. And they're always full of themselves around feeding time. Liverwurst," she scolded the horse, "I'm ashamed of you!"

But Audrey Flowers wasn't listening to her explanations. "Are you all right?" she demanded of Colt.

He nodded, flushed and angry because he knew there were tears on his cheeks.

"Does your back hurt?"

He shook his head, but Audrey was not convinced.

"Does it hurt *at all*?"

"Mom," Colt said, starting to get some of his poise back, "it's too soon for it to hurt."

In fact he felt weak and achy all over. His mother looked hard at him, then turned to Mrs. Reynolds. "I believe I'd better take him home."

"Whatever you think is best," said Mrs. Reynolds quietly. "I'm very sorry this happened."

Colt did not look at Liverwurst as Mrs. Reynolds and his mother got him off the saddle and into the car.

Audrey Flowers did not say much in the car on the way home. She had her serious, wait-and-see look on, and she drove carefully, as if afraid of hurting something. At supper she told Brad about the trotting incident in quiet tones that fooled no one: Audrey was upset. Colt ate his supper without saying much—he didn't know what to say. He went to bed early, lay in the dark, and begged whatever authority was in charge of spina bifida to please not let his back act up.

It was no use. The throbbing of his lump woke him early in the morning.

His mother came into his bedroom as soon as she heard him thump down headfirst from his bed. "How's the back?"

"Fine, Mom." He scooter-boarded past her toward the bathroom, not looking at her. She followed him.

"Does it hurt *at all*?" she yelled at him through the door.

Colt managed to convince her he was all right until time for Sunday breakfast, when she noticed how stiffly he was sitting in his wooden kitchen chair, how he was not letting its rungs touch his back. She laid down her fork and gave him a hard look. "I'm taking you straight to Dr. DeMieux," she said.

Colt sighed. The spina bifida specialist at the medical center was not going to be happy to see him between regular visits. On a Sunday, yet.

Not that Dr. DeMieux said much. She pursed her lips and inspected the critical area of his back. Lying on his belly on her examining table, Colt swiveled his head around to see if she looked somber. She did. "Inflamed," she said. She prescribed medication. "What have you been doing, Colt?"

"Exercises," he said.

"Horseback riding," his mother said.

"It was just the trotting," Colt protested.

"Don't you remember I specified no trotting when I signed permission for your horseback riding?" Dr. DeMieux looked perturbed.

Colt faltered, "But that was just for, like, the summer program. I've been taking private lessons. I'm a lot-better rider now."

"It does not matter. If your horse is going to trot,

I am afraid I have to say, Colt, that you must not ride horseback anymore."

Obviously she did not understand. All he had to do was make her understand and it would be all right. "But I've got to ride," he told her, calmly explaining. "I love riding, especially trail riding. I won't let Liverwurst trot with me anymore until I've really learned to post. I—"

"Young man, it's your life we're talking about here," Dr. DeMieux interrupted.

"Yes," Colt said, a stubborn edge nudging into his voice. "It is."

"Colt!" his mother warned. "He's getting a mind of his own," she said, apologizing to the doctor.

"That's all right. But in that case he must learn to reason things out." Dr. DeMieux sat down on her rolling stool so that she faced Colt at eye level. "Colt. You have heard certain things before, but think what they really mean. When I say it is your life, I mean that little mass protruding from your spine: It is your life. If you make it sore, if you cause more nerve damage, then a little bit of you dies. If you rub it open and it becomes infected, there is nothing to keep the infection from entering your spinal cord and going straight to your brain. You could die."

Colt swallowed hard but said, "Anytime I walk I could fall down and hurt myself, break my neck and die."

"This is true. But on horseback you are twice as

far from the ground as when you walk. If you fall,
you will hurt yourself twice as badly. And you have
seen what happened when you didn't even fall! No
more horseback riding."

It was no use talking to Dr. DeMieux.

The car was very silent on the way home. Colt
sat scared silent. Never ride horseback again? It was
unthinkable. Horseback riding was the one thing that
made him feel complete, whole, really alive. He had
to do something, say something to keep his horseback riding, and he knew his life—the life he wanted
to live—depended on it.

"Mom," he begged, "don't pay attention to Dr.
DeMieux. Please. She doesn't understand."

His mother sighed, stared straight ahead over the
steering wheel, and said nothing. She was driving
slowly. Colt knew she had to be feeling almost as
bad as he did, to be so silent, to be driving so slowly.

"Mom," he tried again, "of course she said not to
ride. She's a doctor. She'd like me to never do anything."

All his mother said was, "Let me sleep on it, Colt."

He slept before she did. The medication made him
groggy. He went to bed right after lunch and lay
there, too doped to feel awake, too heartsick to really
sleep. He heard his mother on the phone with
somebody who must have been Mrs. Reynolds:
"Please don't feel bad. You know what they say:
hindsight's twenty-twenty . . . I guess horses are like
kids, full of surprises. Colt wants to come back and

try it again, but I'm not so sure . . . Uh-huh . . . Might the horse trot with him again when he's not expecting it? Yes . . . So there's no way of being certain the horse won't trot with him . . . I see . . . well, thank you for everything. I'll let you know what we decide."

Mom, please . . .

Later he heard her talking with Brad. "He's been so—so grown-up about this horseback-riding thing, that's what breaks my heart. That's the main reason I let him do it in the first place, because of the way he asked. For once he didn't whine."

Brad's deep voice: "And he hasn't whined or asked for much since."

"And all the exercising he's done, the way he's gotten so much more strength and endurance . . . I could just cry."

Don't cry, Colt thought blurrily. *Just say I can ride.*

"But it's just not safe," said his mother as if she had heard him. "I mean, I know nothing's ever truly safe. But horseback riding—it's like you said, it's really risky. He could fall, or get thrown—"

"Not so likely with a calm horse," said Brad.

Colt decided that he loved Brad.

"But what I can't see worth a darn," Brad said slowly, "is how he's supposed to learn to trot without getting joggled. It doesn't seem possible."

Colt changed his mind—he hated Brad.

"Dammit," Brad said. "I wish I could give him my back and legs."

Because he couldn't hate Brad anymore, Colt began silently to cry.

He went all the way to sleep sometime soon after, and slept through supper. His mother woke him to give him medication, and after that he slept through the night. He woke up late the next morning and realized he was not going to school. And his mother must have taken off work to stay home with him, because in a minute she came into his bedroom and looked at him, and he lay in his bed looking back at her.

"How's the back? Does it still hurt?"

"Mom, it's fine."

"Right. Sure. You told me that yesterday."

He couldn't stand it any longer. "Mom, please . . ."

She came over to him at once, crouched down and held his face between her hands. "Colt," she said, "no. I'm sorry, but no. No more riding. You're my only kid. I can't risk losing you."

Chapter Six

"Want to play rummy or something?" Lauri offered.

"No thanks." It was more than two months since that last disastrous ride; it was November, nearly Thanksgiving, and Colt still didn't feel like doing anything. It was not that he was sulking. He felt too miserable to enjoy sulking. He wasn't even interested in being a brat anymore.

Lauri said more quietly, "Want to talk?"

He had talked with her before, and knew she understood better than most people because she loved horses. She could imagine how he felt about Liverwurst. She had stopped being one of those strange, alien, interesting beings called "girl" and had turned into a friend. But there were some things maybe she couldn't understand. Colt was not sure she could imagine how it felt to be a boy, and handicapped. How someday he was going to want a girl to like him as a boy, and he wasn't sure it could ever happen. . . . He shook his head. "What's to talk about?"

Lauri shrugged. "Well, I've got to do my math."

Rosie drifted into the bedroom as Lauri left. Cross-country season was over, the hair had long since grown back on Rosie's legs, and now he wore sweat pants anyway. He said to Colt, "Play you a game of chess?"

Colt didn't even have the energy to be annoyed at invitations that were getting repetitious. "No. Thanks."

Rosie got down on the floor, stretched, and said, "Do some exercises with me?"

Lying on his bed, Colt did not even shrug. Rosie looked at him.

"No use letting yourself lose all that muscle tone you got last summer, even if you can't go horseback riding anymore."

"I hate exercises," Colt said without much spirit. All his life he had been doing physical therapy, and all his life he was going to be doing physical therapy, by the looks of things. And he had never been able to enjoy exercises for their own sake. He had to have a reason to want to do them.

"Hey, superjock, you should learn to like them," Rosie tried to tease. "Girls love muscles. Especially push-up muscles."

"Give me a break," Colt said bitterly. "No girl's ever going to want me." This was maybe not quite true. Once he had dreamed of having his own car with hand controls and a girl to ride around in it with him. But now he didn't want to dream about anything.

Silence. Then Rosie protested quietly, "Aw, Colt, c'mon. Wake up. Things could be worse."

Colt was convinced that they couldn't be. Suddenly he was angry, and he reared up and blazed at the older boy, "You don't know what it's like! I've got to live like this. . . . You want to know how bad spina bifida is? It's so bad they don't even know how long I'm supposed to last!"

Rosie's eyes widened. What Colt meant was that treatment had come so far so fast the statistics were not yet in. But Colt didn't explain this to Rosie. Explaining would have spoiled the effect.

"And right now I really don't care!"

"Yes you do," said Rosie from the floor.

"No I don't! Why should I care about anything? My own father—" Colt stopped with a gulp. He hadn't meant to talk about that.

Rosie looked at him. "Go ahead," Rosie said, and in response to his quiet tone Colt did.

"After I was born, he left. Disappeared. Never came back. Didn't want to have anything to do with me. Doesn't even want to look at me because I'm such a freak. Now, isn't that supposed to make me feel good?" Colt's voice rose to a cynical whine.

"Could be worse," Rosie said. "My mom left for no particular reason at all."

Colt grew still, looking at Rosie. Something hidden behind Rosie's words told him that "could be worse" was not just an expression people used. Rosie's mom had left when Rosie was old enough to miss her. Maybe it really had been worse for Rosie.

"Sorry," Colt muttered.

"Sure, let's have a pity party." Rosie grimaced, making fun of himself, but kept talking just the same. "You want to know what I hate the worst of all? The name she gave me. My real name, I mean." He looked up at Colt and quirked a sour smile. "Hey? Would it cheer you up if I told you what it is? Want a good laugh?"

Colt just looked at him.

"It's Francis," Rosie told him. "Francis Tewksbury Flowers."

"Lord," said Colt, but he didn't laugh.

Rosie had not done any exercises after all. He got up, retreated across the room, and flopped on his studio couch. "Hey, Rosie," Colt called to him.

"What?" Rosie sounded gruff.

"I can beat that. My real name is Osvaldo."

"It's *what*?"

"Osvaldo Alfonso Vittorio."

Their eyes met across the room, and suddenly they were both laughing like a pair of loons.

By Thanksgiving Colt had thought, grudgingly, of a few things to be thankful for. He was thankful that he had a different school aide this year and she was nice, with a sense of humor, not a fussbudget. He was thankful that his mother and Brad were happy together. He was thankful that the chaos in the Flowers–Vittorio household had subsided somewhat, and that Muffins had finally stopped barking at the new family members. He was thankful that he had Rosie and Lauri for friends, and that Lauri brought girlfriends home with her, and that some of them were almost his friends too. They liked to talk about horses with him. They said most boys didn't know about horses the way he did. Some of them had even started saying hi to him in school.

"I am thankful that I'm back on day work," said Brad at the Thanksgiving dinner table. "And I'm thankful that Lauri has switched to an evening paper route."

"Hear, hear," said Audrey.

Right after Thanksgiving Colt began to consider what he was going to get everyone for Christmas, and how he was going to manage it. He had never had so many people to buy for before. His mother would probably give him some money to shop with, but he wanted to get Rosie something really nice. And Brad. And sure, Lauri too.

Coming home from school the first day after Thanksgiving vacation, he saw Lauri's stack of newspapers waiting for her on the front sidewalk, and he got an idea. Colt got home earlier than Lauri because he was delivered to his door by a special school van, while she had to take the regular bus.

·COLT·

So she would be along later, and when Lauri had to deliver papers and had lessons or a lot of homework too, her day really got crowded. Sometimes she complained about how long the papers took. Colt resented her complaining, because he considered her lucky to have two strong legs so she could make money for herself. But it did take her until after dark sometimes to get her route all delivered. Maybe . . .

Colt made his way into the house and got the things he needed. When Lauri got home she found Colt on the front sidewalk rubber-banding her newspapers and packing them into the carrying bags for her.

"Hey, Colt, thanks!" Lauri was so astonished she stammered. "I—I— this is the first nice thing that's happened all day. Now I'll get done in time to watch a little TV before I have to struggle with social studies."

Colt felt embarrassed by her gratitude. "I'm not being nice," he mumbled. "I thought maybe—oh, forget it." He'd just do the blasted rubber-banding for her once in a while.

She dropped her books to the concrete with a thunk, squatted down, and looked at him. "You thought maybe what?"

She had her stubborn look on. Already Colt knew about Lauri's stubborn look. He gave in.

"I thought maybe if I did this for you every day, you'd give me some of your collections money."

Rather than being disappointed in him, she looked

happier than ever. She jumped up, did a small dance, then stuck out her hand at him. "Give me five, partner! Every day? I'm in heaven!" She slapped hands with him, grabbed the bag he had ready for her, and skylarked off to do part of her route.

Colt felt kind of good for almost the first time since "No Horseback Riding."

A week later Lauri gave him his share of her pay. "What are you going to do with your wealth, moneybags?" she teased.

"Christmas is coming," Colt told her. "Hey. What do you think I ought to get your dad?"

"Gee, I dunno. I haven't thought much about Christmas yet."

But Brad must have been thinking about it. Or rather, Brad seemed to have an uncanny ability to know what Colt was thinking. That Saturday, while Colt was watching cartoons, Brad wandered into the living room. "Colt," he proposed, "how's about I give you a few dollars every week for doing some things around the house?"

Colt tore his attention away from the TV and blinked at Brad. He had always considered the house his mother's responsibility, because she seemed to think it was. "I am such a mess," she would declare, as if the clutter surrounding her was all her fault. But Brad seemed to think otherwise.

"Thing is," he was saying, "we should all lend a hand. But Rosie and Lauri just aren't home as much as you are, and neither am I. And your mom is going to be working overtime now that Christmas is coming. If we're going to get this place cleaned up for the holidays, you're the one who's going to have to do a lot of it. And it seems to me that if you're going to do more than the rest of us, I should pay you."

"Sure," said Colt. "Okay." Though in fact he was not sure how much he *could* do around the house. He had never tried.

It turned out he could do plenty. A kid on a scooter board, he discovered that weekend, can sweep and wash a kitchen floor with a lot less back strain than a standing-up adult. A kid in leg braces can push a vacuum cleaner. A kid in a wheelchair can carry junk mail to the trash. Colt could clear the table, even set the table. About the only thing he couldn't do was climb on a stepladder to wash windows.

By the time Christmas came, Colt was smiling again. Sometimes.

He hadn't seen much of his mother and Brad for most of December. They were working hard, and (he sensed) busy with their own secrets. But of course they had taken him shopping, and he had had a wonderful time trundling all over the mall in his wheelchair, spending his wealth. He got Brad some really good fur-lined leather gloves, and Rosie a brand-name sweat suit (along with a rubber snake to surprise him when he opened the package), and Lauri special socks guaranteed to keep her feet warm no matter what sort of ridiculous weather she was delivering newspapers in. He got his mother a fuzzy bathrobe and a cuddly plush unicorn to sit on her pillow. Everybody liked the things he got them, and he liked all the things he got, including the rubber snake Rosie had put in *his* package.

Christmas afternoon after dinner Brad came out of the kitchen carrying an apple and a carrot and said, "C'mon, Colt. C'mon, everybody. We're going to wish Mrs. Reynolds and Liverwurst a Merry Christmas."

Colt looked at Brad, feeling the old ache in his heart. It had never been gone, not really. Maybe it never would be. Though Christmas or something seemed to have made it ease up quite a bit.

"Don't you think Liverwurst should have a Christmas treat?" Brad asked him.

"Yeah," said Colt, "sure," and he wobbled to his feet. No need to switch from braces and crutches to wheelchair, as he usually did when he would be riding so he didn't have to struggle out of the braces before he got on the horse. No need, because he wouldn't be riding.

Four Flowerses and one Vittorio piled into the car to go out to Deep Meadows Farm, and it didn't occur to Colt to wonder why everyone was coming along. It was Christmas, a family day. Naturally this family would do things as a family.

Colt forgot he had ever felt angry and hurt at Liverwurst the moment he saw that familiar ugly head thrust out over the stall door. "Hey, Liverwurst!"

he called in greeting, and he walked, crutches whirling, at top speed down the stable aisle. It was good to be standing up, to be able to cuddle Liverwurst's head against his chest and lean his cheek against Liverwurst's wisp of a forelock. He slipped off his crutches so he could use his hands, steadied himself against the stall door, and rubbed Liverwurst's cheekbones. Liverwurst smelled the apple in his jacket pocket and nosed at it, hinting. Colt fed it to him, and then the carrot. "Merry Christmas, Liverwurst," he said huskily. "How you been?"

"He's been fine, but he's missed you." It was Janet Reynolds, in blue jeans even on Christmas day, smiling at him across the stable aisle. "How are you, Colt?"

Coming from her, this was not just a polite thing to say. She was really asking. "I'm okay," Colt said.

And then he saw.

In the stall beside her, a horse he had never seen on her farm before.

Even though he could see only the head and neck, it was, he knew at once, the prettiest horse he had ever seen off a TV screen. It had a delicate, gentle face the color of old gold, with a wide starred forehead between eyes like the nighttime sky. Over the eyes cascaded a silver waterfall of forelock. A mass of mane of the same brilliant silver flowed down the horse's neck, and in it Colt saw stirrings of red and green where thin Christmas-colored tendrils of ribbon were wound into the forelock and mane and tied in tiny bows at the horse's arched crest. It looked like a horse out of a Christmas dream, all gift-gold and moon-silver and starlight sparkle in the eyes—so beautiful Colt gawked and leaned against Liverwurst for support.

"What—what horse is that?" he gasped.

Instead of answering, Mrs. Reynolds opened the stall door and led the horse out with just a rope looped around its neck. She brought it over to where it could snuffle Colt. It was a small horse, not much bigger than a big pony, and its body had a soft, round, graceful look. Even in velvety winter fur, its brown-gold haunches were faintly mottled with dapples. It was all of that rich color except for its heavy silver mane and tail, its star and its small hooves. They were clay-gray and unshod, and Colt noticed that when the little horse walked, it seemed to glide like a dancer, nearly crossing its feet in the front.

"Her name is Bonita," Mrs. Reynolds said. "She's a Paso Fino. The color is called 'chocolate palomino.' "

Colt's mother and Brad and Rosie and Lauri were standing in a cluster not far away, all watching, all smiling, looking content just to let Colt pat a horse on Christmas—which was all he was ever going to be able to do with horses again: pat them.

Bonita smelled the carrot juice on Colt and nuzzled his hand. He felt sorry he did not have a treat left for her.

"She's *beautiful*," he told Mrs. Reynolds. "Is she

yours?" She might have belonged to someone else. Mrs. Reynolds kept a few horses belonging to other people at her farm.

"If you want to see whose she is," said Mrs. Reynolds, "you'd better read the card."

Card? She pointed it out to him. Tied onto a ribbon, it hung nearly hidden in Bonita's thick mane.

If this is some kind of joke . . .

Colt didn't dare look at anyone as he reached for the card with a shaking hand, trying not to think what he knew had to be impossible. This horse was a Christmas gift? For him? But that couldn't be. They wouldn't give him a horse. They knew he wanted to ride, and he couldn't ride after the damage Liverwurst had done by trotting with him just a little. He was handicapped, and he had to remember that.

I'm being stupid, I'm missing something. I can't ride horseback. It was dumb ever to think I could ride horseback. Stupid even to think this horse might be for me.

"Come on," his mother urged, "open it!" She was standing close by, smiling, and Brad had his arm around her and was grinning like mad.

Got to be some kind of joke. Try to be a good sport. Try not to cry or do anything dumb. . . .

Colt had to lean against Liverwurst's stall door while his shaking hands tore at the card. He felt weak all over.

It just couldn't be . . .

It was.

The card said:

To Colt,
Merry Christmas!
Happy Trails!
THIS HORSE DOES NOT TROT!

Love,
Mom, Brad, Rosie, and Lauri.

Chapter Seven

"We would have told you sooner," Colt's mother explained to him after the hugging and laughing and sniffling and more hugging were over, "but we didn't want to get your hopes up. We weren't sure it would work out. It had to be a very special horse."

"Mom, thank you so much." Tears wet Colt's cheeks, but for once he didn't mind. "I don't know how to thank you enough."

"Thank Brad. I had never even *heard* of a Paso Fino."

Brad had gotten him Bonita? Colt looked at him, and Brad looked away, embarrassed. "It's just that when I was in the service in Puerto Rico we used to ride these incredible little horses. They don't ever trot, or even gallop unless you make them. They just walk faster and faster."

"I couldn't believe it until I saw it," Colt's mother put in.

"Anyhow, when my old C.O. moved back to Ohio, he took a few Pasos with him, and now he raises them. He always was quite a horseman."

Brad seemed talked out. Audrey prompted, "So after we talked it over, Brad wrote him—"

"And I gave Daddy some of my newspaper money," Lauri put in. "And Rosie gave him some—"

"Shut up," Rosie grumbled. He looked as sheepish as his father.

"And we asked him to find us a very gentle, well-schooled Paso at a price we could afford," Brad continued. "Not asking much, huh? But he managed to do it." Colt stood rubbing Bonita's starred forehead, and Brad grinned at him like a shy kid. "Turned out he was looking for a good home for Bonita all along." Brad pulled a much-folded letter out of his shirt pocket and passed it over for Colt to read:

Dear Brad,

Good to hear from you after all these years! I am glad to hear you have remarried and you're happy with your new wife and family.

I may have the very horse for the little guy you mention. A mare with some age on her, Bonita, a Splendifico daughter. Beautiful conformation. We thought we were going to make a show horse out of her, so she has been very well trained, but she had such a quiet disposition even as a filly that she never placed well. No *brio.* No fire. She's a wonderful pleasure Paso, stays in frame under any rider, so I could have sold her to someone for trail riding, but I would have taken a licking. She's small, too small for a big rider, and all people can think about these days is size, size, size! Anyway, I wanted some foals from her. Turned out she's no good as a brood mare either. Doesn't "take." But I think she might be perfect for your youngster. She's unusually quiet, dead safe with any rider, and smooth as silk in her gait. Give me a call and we'll make arrangements to send her to you for a month's trial. I'll pay the shipping. As a matter of fact I've got half a mind to give you the horse outright, since it's for such a good cause, but I know you're too darn proud. Once you've tried Bonita, if she suits you, just name your price and whatever you say will be okay with me. And send me a few photos of the kid on her.

The letter was signed "Tick" and was on the stationery of the Ticknor Family Paso Fino Farm. Colt decided that he profoundly liked Mr. Ticknor. He would write Mr. Ticknor a letter before anyone had to tell him to do it.

"Wow," he said. He looked up to pass the letter back to Brad, and found himself facing a camera lens. All the questions he had been going to ask focused into one: the one big question.

"Can I ride her?" he demanded, his voice rocketing out of control. "Today?"

Everyone was smiling, and he knew the answer was yes—with one condition.

"Only if I walk beside you, Colt," Mrs. Reynolds spoke up. "You're going to have to start from scratch. You've let yourself lose all your riding muscle!"

Half an hour later, after helping to saddle and bridle Bonita and after shedding his leg braces, Colt was on Bonita having his picture taken for Mr. Ticknor. He knew he was wearing a big, undignified grin under his helmet, and he didn't care. It was the best Christmas ever.

January and February went by in fast-forward for Colt. He had work to do, and he was happy to do it. Newspapers to rubber-band for Lauri; housework to keep up with; schoolwork (He tried hard to pay attention in school, knowing that if he got behind he would have to spend extra time with homework and tutoring, which was time he would rather spend with Bonita); and exercises. Every day he did exercises to strengthen his back and legs. In the spring, once the weather had warmed up and Mrs. Reynolds felt sure he was strong enough, he would ride Bonita out on the trail.

Weekly he had lessons on her in the ring. He had to learn to ride all over again. Everything was different with the little Paso Fino.

"Whoa!" he yelled the first time she scooted six

feet sideways with him. The motion, though smooth as glass, frightened him breathless.

"You touched her with your right leg," Mrs. Reynolds explained. "She's trained to move away from the slightest pressure. Your legs are getting stronger than they were before, and she thought you wanted her to side-pass."

"Wow," said Colt. If he had touched Liverwurst accidentally, Liverwurst would have done nothing but twitch as if a fly were itching him.

"It's good she's so sensitive," Mrs. Reynolds added, "because your signals will never be strong, no matter how much you exercise those legs of yours. You just have to learn how to ride her, that's all. She's like a fine-tuned machine."

Colt rode Bonita forward. Her side-pass had made him a little nervous, because it felt like being shied with. That was one thing he was afraid of: What might happen if a horse shied with him? Would he be able to stay on? Or would he fall?

His anxious thoughts affected his hands. Instead of keeping light contact with Bonita's mouth as he usually did, he tightened up on the reins.

Bonita surged forward.

Slick as a cat the little mare glided into a quick, collected, four-beat gait. Colt felt only a faint vibration, as if he were riding in the backseat of a Cadillac, but suddenly the fence posts of the riding ring were whirling past at a speed he had never experienced before. His head and shoulders and back and seat rode steady as the little horse motored along, paca-paca-paca-paca, underneath him. Bonita performed the *paso corto* with her pretty chin tucked, the white star on her forehead shining straight forward, the silver mane stirring on her arched neck. Colt forgot to be afraid. He felt as if he were flying, skimming the world on wings. He felt weightless. He felt—free.

"Beautiful!" Mrs. Reynolds called. "When did you learn how to gait her, Colt?"

"I didn't!"

"I see. Well, if you want her to slow down, just loosen the reins."

Colt did so, and Bonita slowed to the easy walk he was used to.

"The faster you want her to go," Mrs. Reynolds explained as he brought her to a stop, "the more you gather her in."

Colt blinked dizzily. Everything was backward with the Paso Fino. If he wanted Bonita to go left, he pressed with his right knee. If he wanted her to back up, he leaned forward. If he wanted her to go forward, he leaned back. If he wanted her to go faster, he tightened the reins.

He loved riding her.

"I want to be sure you understand, Colt," Mrs. Reynolds said to him seriously, "that you cannot ride just any horse. Even with gaited horses, you must be very careful what you ride. Some horses might be well trained but if they have a mean streak they will still take advantage of you and hurt you. Stick to Bonita. You are as safe on her as you can ever be on horseback, and that's not only because of her smooth gait but because she is a very gentle, responsive, good-hearted horse. She is special."

Colt knew that, and was grateful.

After the lesson he helped Mrs. Reynolds groom Bonita. Sitting in his wheelchair, he could brush Bonita's belly and legs more easily than Janet Reynolds could. He was learning to lift Bonita's feet and remove the dirt from her small oval hooves with a hoof pick. After the grooming was done, he watched Mrs. Reynolds put Bonita in a paddock with Liverwurst.

Always before, Liverwurst had needed to stay in a paddock by himself. Even though he was as big as any horse on the farm, he let himself be picked on. Whenever Mrs. Reynolds put him out in the main pasture, ponies half his size would kick him and drive him away from water and food, and he would not defend himself. If he had been kept with the herd, he would always have been covered with bites and bruises. But Bonita did not bite him, and she had become his paddock mate.

Liverwurst trotted to meet her at the gate, nickering, nuzzling at her neck. Bonita swiveled her ears to a bored sideward position and swung her head away from the big, pesky gelding, but did not squeal or kick. She moved away from Liverwurst and started to graze, and Mrs. Reynolds laughed.

"She's very sweet with him. She puts up with a lot of nonsense from him. Liverwurst doesn't know how to act. I believe she's his first love."

"Liverwurst has a girlfriend," Colt sang.

The big, blotchy Appaloosa did not seem to mind. He poked at Bonita with his huge nose and awaited a reaction, looking wide-eyed and anxious, as always. Bonita, ignoring him, seemed, more than ever, dainty and aristocratic next to him, like a princess being pestered by a goblin.

"Beauty and the beast," Mrs. Reynolds remarked to Colt's mother, who had come to pick him up. "He's devoted to her."

"Poor Bonita," said Audrey.

"Aw!" Colt protested. "Liverwurst isn't a beast. Well, not the way you mean."

Mrs. Reynolds said, "He's a big, homely, very sweet beast."

One day after school there was a large package waiting along with the newspapers on the doorstep, and it had Colt's name on it.

"What the heck?" he remarked with interest, and then with even greater interest he saw the return address: Ticknor Family Paso Fino Farm, Bluesville, Ohio. "Oh, wow!" He knew it had to be something good.

It was. When Lauri came home she did not mind doing her own rubber-banding for once, because Colt was sitting with one hand on his new saddle, read-

·COLT·

ing Mr. Ticknor's letter and looking dangerously wet around the eyes. The letter said,

Dear Colt,

An old horseman has to like a kid with such a name. Also I have very much enjoyed your letters and the photos of you on Bonita. I am sorry not to have answered your letters sooner. But better late than never, and here is something I think you will like.

I see from the photos that you are riding Bonita on an all-purpose English saddle and using a snaffle bit. The snaffle is fine. Stick with it. Any horse that needs a bit stronger than a snaffle is not the horse for you. But it seems to me that a horse of Spanish breeding such as Bonita looks nice under a Spanish saddle, and also that such a saddle, having a high pommel and cantle, would give you more support. So here is one. I would have sent it along in the first place except I knew that ornery critter, Brad, would want to pay me for it. Now it is just a gift from me to you, and he can forget about getting his wallet out. You can tell him I said so.

You need a wool blanket under the saddle, and I've included one for you. It goes on the horse first. The leather pad goes over that, and then the saddle on top of the pad, which acts as a skirt to distribute your weight. The sheepskin goes on top of the saddle to give you a softer seat and keep the saddle leather un-

·87

scratched. The stirrups, as you can see, are wooden and fasten onto the saddle by billets that can be shortened or lengthened.

I have sent along a Spanish bridle also. Just use it with a plain snaffle bit.

This saddle is probably fifty years old, but you can see it looks almost new. Keep it lubricated with neat's-foot oil and it will stay that way. You can polish the silverwork with a soft rag. I hope you'll send me another snapshot and let me know how the new saddle is working.

Yrs, Tick.

The saddle, with its rich dark leather and silver studding, and the bridle, exquisitely braided and tooled and decorated with buttons of silver, were so beautiful Colt could not stop looking at them. He could not believe Mr. Ticknor had sent him such wonderful things just out of the goodness of his heart. Yet when he thought about it he realized that all his life people had been doing things for him out of the goodness of their hearts: Horseback Riding for the Handicapped volunteers, teachers, therapists, Mrs. Reynolds, his mother.

Colt did not know what Mr. Ticknor looked like. He decided to ask Mr. Ticknor for a photo of himself. He suspected that Mr. Ticknor, like Liverwurst, was a big, homely, very kind creature.

The saddle worked beautifully. It had a cantle that stood up three or four inches and curved to enclose

·COLT·

Colt almost like the back of a chair, but did not interfere with his lump. It did, indeed, give him a more secure seat on Bonita. Mrs. Reynolds was pleased to report after a couple of weeks that Colt was riding more strongly than ever. He could guide Bonita from walk to *paso corto* to *paso largo* and back again with ease. He could back her, side-pass her, and turn her on her haunches, no problem. He was more than ready to ride out on the trail.

March came and turned Pennsylvania to mud. As soon as the ground dried in the warm spring wind, it would be time for Colt to get out of the ring and into the woodlands he remembered from that single trail ride the past summer.

"I can't *wait*," he told his mother. She was washing the supper dishes, he was drying them, and Rosie was putting them away.

"I bet," said his mother. She had been along on that trail ride too, as one of Jay Gee's side walkers, he remembered. And she actually seemed to sense something of what those hushed high-pine woodlands meant to her son. "If we had another horse as nice as Bonita, I'd take time off from work and come with you."

"You?! You would?"

She gave him a smile. "Tell you a secret. I wasn't sure about letting you have Bonita at first. So as soon as she came, Brad put me on her."

"You rode Bonita!"

"Sure did. Several times. I figured if I could ride her and not get in trouble, anybody could."

"Anyway," Brad called from the next room, "I didn't want to ride her myself. She's little. I was afraid I'd be too heavy for her."

"Sheesh!" Colt was grinning. "So how long were you two playing around with my horse before I got her?"

"Long enough to know that she's too fast for me to walk along beside," said Audrey Flowers. "And you're never to ride her by yourself, young man," she added sternly.

Colt knew that. He had already discussed trail riding with Mrs. Reynolds. Someday soon she was going to saddle up her own horse and ride out with him.

"Heck, I could run along with you, Ozzie," said Rosie, half joking.

"Right, Frannie."

"You think I'm kidding? I bet that pony of yours couldn't keep up with me."

Colt flicked him with the dish towel.

Chapter Eight

Colt did not know until a few days afterward how grateful to be for Rosie's offer.

The phone call came in during supper. Colt, eating, heard only his mother's end of the conversation. "Hello? No, that's all right, Janet, we were just finishing . . . Oh, dear, I'm sorry to hear that. Colt will be sorry too . . . Well, I hope you're feeling better real soon. If you need any help when you get home, please give us a call . . . now stop worrying, Colt will survive."

Survive WHAT?

When Colt's mother came back to the kitchen after a few more minutes of telling Mrs. Reynolds to take care of herself and concentrate on getting well, she found that her son had lost all interest in his spaghetti. Colt knew he was about to hear something he wouldn't like.

"Janet has to go into the hospital for some surgery," Mrs. Flowers reported to the family. "No riding lessons for a while, Colt. Even after she gets out she'll have to take it easy for several weeks.

"Several *weeks*?" Colt knew now that he would not survive.

"What kind of surgery?" asked Lauri at the same time. Colt's outburst, being louder, got answered first.

"Good grief, Colt, don't yell. It's not as if you can't ride at all. You're to ride whenever you can. Janet made quite a point of that. She said you will be fine on the horse. One of us is to be with you, that's all."

"What kind of surgery?" asked Lauri.

"But we were going on the *trail* soon!" wailed Colt.

"Colt, stop sounding like a brat. We'll see what we can do," said his mother. Colt wanted to scream. The we'll-see-what-we-can-do meant his mother felt hassled and didn't want to be bothered. After all the time he had waited he was going to have to wait some more. . . .

Lauri asked again, "What kind of surgery?"

"What's it to you?" Colt shouted at her. "Sheesh!"

"I just wondered if maybe she had cancer or something."

"What makes you think it's gotta be cancer!"

"Colt, quiet down or go to your room," his mother

ordered. "I didn't ask her what kind of surgery, Lauri. That's personal."

"But didn't she say?"

"You're sick, you know that?" Colt raged at Lauri. "Sick!"

"Colt," his mother told him, "that's enough. I'm not going to even talk with you about riding until you *calm down*."

He did, gradually. It took him a few days. But by Saturday morning he was able to scooter-board calmly into his mother's bedroom (she was combing her hair) and say to her in level and civil tones, "Mom, it's beautiful outside. May I go riding?"

"Colt, I have to go to work." She worked alternate Saturdays. The next one, it would probably be raining. "Maybe tomorrow," she added. Sunday. It always rained on Sundays, didn't she know that?

"Mom, *please*," said Colt, carefully keeping his voice down. He knew he was being unreasonable. He could not really expect her to skip work. Brad was working too, overtime, he knew that. But there was one other person, who had probably been joking . . .

He asked, "How about if Rosie takes me?"

"Well, I don't know . . ." Rosie had just gotten his driver's license the week before. "He might not even want to take you, Colt. I think he was just kidding when he said he would."

"I don't think so," said Colt, even though he

did. "Rosie!" He scooted off to find the lanky teen-ager.

Rosie seemed to have grown six inches since fall, and it showed in the way he moved. His head, hands, and feet seemed always to be surprising him by being farther from the rest of him than he expected. When Colt found him, he was keeping himself out of trouble by daydreaming on his studio couch. His feet hung over the end, looking gigantic in new running shoes.

"Rosie. Take me riding today? Before it starts to rain again?"

"I got to go to the mall and meet a girl," said Rosie without looking at Colt.

"Aw! Pleeeze?"

Then Rosie turned his head, and Colt saw his grin, and knew he had been teasing, and wanted to hit him.

"*Rosie*—"

"Okay, okay! I need to run anyway." With a huge sigh Rosie heaved himself up from his bed.

"You mean . . ." Colt scarcely dared to believe it. "You mean we're going out on the trail?"

"Sure, Ozzie. Where else?"

However, neither of them mentioned that detail of their plan to Colt's mother as they dropped her off at work. They didn't want to worry her. Even as it was, she kept telling Rosie to drive safely and reminding Colt to wear his helmet.

Rosie drove safely, but he and Colt joked all the

way out to the stable. Something giddy was in the air. It was just what Colt had said: a beautiful day. More than beautiful—it was magnificent, glorious, exciting in the way that only an early-spring day of sunshine and warm breeze can be after a long winter's drear. It was a day that promised good things to come forever.

There was nobody home at Deep Meadows Farm when they arrived except, of course, the horses in their paddocks and pastures. Mr. Reynolds might have been at the hospital visiting his wife. None of the other boarders happened to be there to ride so early in the day.

Rosie helped Colt out of the car and into his wheelchair, then led Bonita in from the pasture by a big soft rope around her neck. Colt had to tell him what to do to get her ready to ride, and he looked very out of place in his sweats, gym shorts, and running shoes as he brushed off Bonita's back. He moved stiffly around the little mare, keeping an eye on her even though she was doing nothing but standing placidly, her pretty head nodding.

"Pick up her feet and get the crud out of them," Colt directed.

"Are you kidding? What if she kicks me?"

"Oh, for crying out loud. Give me the hoof pick. I'll do it." Colt took care of the feet from his wheelchair. He did the bridling too, because Rosie did not want to put his hand near Bonita's teeth. Colt could not have bridled a head-tossing horse from his wheelchair, but Bonita put her nose down to where Colt sat and opened her mouth to receive the bit.

"Shut the tack-room door, keep the cats out," ordered Colt. Mrs. Reynolds had told him that stable cats love nothing better than to perch on saddles and scratch the leather with their sharp claws.

"Yes, O Master." Apparently Rosie had not liked Colt's tone. Or perhaps he did not like having so many strange jobs to do.

It was a relief to both Rosie and Colt when the saddle was on Bonita and Colt on the saddle.

"Okay," said Colt when he had checked to make sure the girth was tight, "let's just walk until we get to the park."

"Am I supposed to walk behind you, or in front of you, or what?"

"Mrs. Reynolds said she might spook, because everything will be strange to her. There's no such thing as a totally spook-proof horse. So you're supposed to walk beside her head and grab the bridle if she spooks."

"Great. What if she bites me?"

"*Rosie . . .*" Colt remembered he had once been frightened of Liverwurst and softened his voice. "Rosie. Would you look at her, for gosh sake? She's not going to bite you."

Bonita stood with her big dark eyes half-shut, shaded by long silver lashes. Her forelock reached nearly to her soft toast-colored nose. Her fuzzy, gold fox-pricked ears pointed sideward.

·COLT·

"That's the kind you got to watch," Rosie grumbled. "The quiet ones."

"Just walk, Francis."

They walked up the farm lane to the country road and along it to the park. From his paddock Liverwurst whinnied after them. Bonita did not reply, but nodded along, swishing her silver tail. In his chest Colt felt happiness gathering like helium. In a moment he and Bonita would lift off and soar among the tall pines, up, up, away.

Rosie nodded cautious approval. "Neat," he remarked, his deep voice hushed. "I can see why you like this place, Ozvaldo."

Warm tangy light poured down through the pine boughs, catching on pale dogwoods in bud, on red-tipped maples, on papaw. Squirrels crossed the trail, their tails floating like shadows along the arcs of their leaps. Looking up, Colt saw blue sky; looking down into one damp hollow he saw a mushroom nearly as blue squatting between vivid green fiddleheads of fern. Brown butterflies with a yellow fringe fluttered over the moist ground—it surprised Colt to see them so early in the year. Then deep in the trees, underbrush crashed as a deer leapt. Bonita pricked her ears toward the sound, nothing more. Like Colt, she took in everything wide-eyed, her small hooves eager on the soft springtime earth.

The trail dipped steeply downward, then leveled again to a broad, grassy path along the lakeshore. Bonita had never seen so much water in one place before. She flared her nostrils and snorted at the strange, shining expanse, then listened to Colt's hands on the reins.

"Ready for a run?" Colt asked Rosie.

"Sure."

Colt settled his seat even deeper in the Spanish saddle, gathered the reins, and smoothly Bonita single-footed into the *paso corto.* Her tawny neck arched and her mane lifted and flowed as her hooves tapped out a rapid, even 1-2-3-4 rhythm on the grassy trail. Wood ducks glided on the lake; Bonita and Colt glided along the shoreline just as easily. Rosie jogged beside the horse's head, no longer afraid of the small, softly clattering hooves flashing near his ankles.

"Faster?" Colt inquired happily.

"Sure!"

Colt signaled Bonita, and with a catlike, reaching motion she lengthened stride into the *paso largo.* Rosie was running now, arms pumping, his long legs outstretched. Bonita was skimming along as fast as most pleasure horses can canter, and in the saddle Colt sat as if in an easy chair.

"All *right!*" Rosie approved. "She's doing a six-minute mile for sure. Maybe five. How long can she keep this up?"

"I don't know! I guess we'll find out."

Horse and rider and runner whirled along the shoreline. Within a few minutes, before they really noticed, the land steepened. No longer down near the water, the trail now ran along a hillside, and the blue-green lake water lapped thirty feet below.

"She getting tired yet?" Rosie puffed as the trail continued to slope upward.

"Rosie," Colt teased, "she's not even sweating!" Which was true. Bonita's flexed neck remained dry, her ears pricked calmly forward.

A dove flew up from trailside with a sudden whistling of pointed wings. Bonita flinched and swerved. Automatically Colt's seat shifted to go with her, his hands signaled for her attention with the reins. Bonita straightened herself and gaited on before Rosie could touch the bridle, and Colt breathed deep with relief and joy. His horse had shied, and he had hardly known it happened before it was over. He would call Mrs. Reynolds that evening and tell her. If that was all there was to shying, it was nothing to be afraid of.

"Maybe we'd better slow down," Rosie panted.

"All right," said Colt regretfully, and he brought Bonita back to her slow walk. Breathing heavily, Rosie turned around and looked at her.

"Yazoo. You weren't kidding. She isn't even sweating yet." Rosie walked backward, talking to Colt. "She's something else, you know that? She's really something. I bet you could even talk me into riding—"

"Watch the edge!"

It was too late. One of Rosie's large wayward feet

had strayed too close to the drop at the side of the trail. Just as Colt spoke Rosie set his foot down half on nothing. The ground, damp from recent rains, melted away under the pressure. Ankle twisting, knee buckling, Rosie fell with a hoarse, startled yell. He thought (and so did Colt, pulling Bonita to a halt, watching, stiff with terror) that he was going to crash all the way down the forty-foot drop and into the lake. His hands flew out, clawing at air and saplings, his back dug a damp furrow in the loam, and like a runaway sled he headed straight for a large beech tree, feet first. With a jarring impact Rosie came to a stop a few yards below the trail.

Bonita looked down at him with blinky brown eyes. From her back Colt looked down with considerably more concern.

"Are you all right?"

Rosie groaned and glared by way of answer. On hands and knees he scrabbled his way up the slope and crawled onto the level surface of the trail. Colt wished he could get down and brush the leaves and pine needles and dirt off Rosie and help him get up. He could not, of course. He could only watch.

Rosie put his weight on one foot and tried to stand up. He winced, then tried the other. He looked up at Colt.

"Dammit," he said. "I've wrecked up both of them."

Colt felt his mind shy and swerve. He steadied it

·COLT·

as if steadying a frightened horse. Calm down. Move forward one step at a time. First things first.

"Did you hit your head on anything?"

"Just the ground."

"Did you do anything to your neck or back?"

"No. I don't think so. Just twisted my ankle going over the edge, and then rammed my feet into the tree."

"So you're okay other than that?"

Rosie rolled his eyes. "Other than that? Sure. Other than that I'm just fine."

Chapter Nine

Colt thought for a minute, then walked Bonita forward a few yards, turned her so that she faced toward
home, then took her back to where Rosie sat. He
tightened one knee just a hair, and Bonita side-passed
a step toward Rosie.

"Hey!" Rosie protested from the ground. "What
are you doing?"

"I'm going to stand her practically on top of you.
Grab the girth and see if you can stand up."

"Just what I've always wanted," Rosie complained,
"a horse in my lap."

Colt positioned Bonita, and then halted her. "All
right," he told Rosie, "try it. I hope you cinched the
saddle tight."

Rosie had. He pulled himself up, hanging on first
to the girth, then to the leather saddle skirt, crawling up Bonita as if scaling a wall, and the horse stood

like a stone. "Good girl," Colt told her. "Okay, Rosie, if she walks slow and you lean on her, do you think you can walk?"

"Guess I'm going to have to." It was not likely that anyone else was going to come along and help. There were few people in the park so early in the year. Colt and Rosie had not seen anyone since they started down the lakeside trail.

"Okay. Hang on." Colt eased Bonita into a slow walk.

Without much guidance from Colt the Paso Fino kept her pace very slow, very smooth. Bonita seemed to understand that something was wrong, that extra cooperation was required of her.

"How you doing, Rosie?"

"Not—too—good." Clinging to the saddle near Colt's knee, Rosie was beginning to pant with pain. His face had gone white. Colt stopped the horse.

"You can't walk. Sit down before you fall down."

Rosie stood where he was, hanging on hard. "Maybe—if I could get on her behind you . . ."

Colt considered. He had to help Rosie somehow.

"You weigh almost as much as your dad, right?" he asked slowly. Bonita was too small to carry Mr. Flowers. Bonita would be too small to carry Colt and Rosie without hurting herself.

"Right," said Rosie. "I forgot."

"But if worse comes to worst . . ." Colt felt his eyes stinging at the thought.

"No way," Rosie told him. "Forget it. We're not going to hurt your horse. I'll crawl first."

Colt knew he couldn't crawl all the way back to the stable, not really. He said, "Let's see if we can get you just a little farther, just down to where you can put your feet in the water."

Rosie shifted his grip so that he held onto Bonita's silky mane, then hobbled on. Twice he had to stop. The last several yards he crawled. Already his feet had swollen so badly that he could not undo the knots of his running shoes. As Colt watched anxiously, Rosie sat on the lakeshore and swung his feet into the cold water, shoes and all. He bent over and splashed water on his knees.

"All right," Colt told him, "stay there. I'm going to find us some help." He sent Bonita toward the stable. If he was lucky, one of the other riders would be there. If not, he hoped at least he could reach the phone.

Hang on, Rosie.

There really was no choice but for Colt to go off on his own, and Rosie knew it. "Be careful!" he called after him.

"Got to, man," Colt called back cheerfully, but he meant it.

He walked Bonita most of the way back. It seemed to take forever. Thinking of Rosie sitting there hurt and alone in the middle of nowhere, once in a while he risked a cautious *paso corto*. He did not dare go faster, because now and then Bonita shied at something along the trail, and he felt worried, though not for himself—if he fell off and got himself hurt, nobody would know where to look for Rosie.

He met no one at all in the park, not a hiker on the trail, not a boat on the lake. Leaving the park, turning onto the roadside, he saw a car coming and lifted a hand to flag it down, but Bonita stiffened, ready to spook, and quickly Colt returned his hand to the reins. The man in the car waved at him and kept going.

Stupid! Can't that guy see I'm in trouble? What would a handicapped kid be doing . . .

And then Colt realized: The man did not know he was handicapped. He was so used to thinking of himself in a certain way that for a moment it was as if his world had flipped, had spun upside down, but it made sense. He wore no braces to ride horseback, no crutches, no wheelchair, and his helmet looked much like anyone else's riding helmet. Unless someone really paid attention to his thin, undeveloped legs, when he was on a horse he just looked like—

Jeez, I just look like a kid on a horse.

A kid who was old enough to handle things on his own. And he was going to have to. Already Colt had a feeling what he was going to find at the stable.

Sure enough. Nobody.

No cars were parked in the stable lot but Rosie's. Mr. Reynolds was not back from wherever he had gone, and no other riders had arrived. Colt rode

Bonita into the barn to be sure. No one was there to help Rosie.

Just inside the tack-room door hung the wall phone. He had to reach it.

He could not.

Whoever had put away the boxes of hard hats and the mounting block the autumn before had set them beside the door, exactly in the wrong place beside the door. Bonita could not stand close enough. Colt stretched, until he was afraid he would fall, and could not reach even the doorknob so that he could open the door and head Bonita into it. Another rider, someone who could lean his weight in a stirrup, might have been able to manage. But Colt could not quite do it.

He hated being handicapped, he hated it, he hated it! Anybody else could have just stepped inside the tack-room door, dialed 911 for help, and here he sat, couldn't do the simplest thing . . . Tears coming. Colt gulped them back.

Grow up, Osvaldo. Smarten up.

Things went wrong for regular people sometimes too. Like, what if the phone was out of order? What would he do then? If he couldn't help Rosie one way, he'd have to help him another way. There had to be one. Handicapped people can do things too.

Like think. You gotta think.

He backed Bonita out of the barn and rode her in a slow circle in front of the stable, considering the possibilities. The nearest houses were half a mile away, along the paved road. Ride Bonita out there, shout at doors, try to find someone home? Very risky, with cars whizzing past. Bonita would get used to cars probably in a few more rides, but for today she was going to spook at them, and if Colt got thrown, there would be nobody who knew where Rosie was. Try to flag down another slow-moving car along the dirt road? Same problem. Wait around the stable for somebody to come? Sure, but absolutely the last choice on his list, with Rosie sitting out there hurt. . . . The alternative was for Colt himself somehow to get Rosie out of the woods. All right, so for a long time he had been used to thinking of himself as pretty helpless, but sitting on top of his horse he knew: There had to be something he could do. . . .

Liverwurst stuck his head out over the paddock gate and whinnied at Bonita.

Horses.

Liverwurst.

Half a minute later Colt had Bonita back inside the barn, where the halters and lead ropes hung from a harness hook just inside the big sliding door. Liverwurst's bridle was safe in the tack room, he couldn't get it, but a halter would be better than nothing. He selected the largest one, and a long lead rope. After a moment's thought he took *two* lead ropes and clipped them one onto each side of the halter, like reins. Then he laid the things across the saddle in front of him and headed Bonita toward the paddock gate.

Liverwurst had ambled away. Of course. Horses were like that, Mrs. Reynolds said. Never handy when you wanted them. "Liverwurst!" Colt called.

The Appaloosa raised his big hammer head from his grazing and gave Colt an owlish stare.

"Liverwurst!"

The new spring grass was more important. The gelding lowered his nose to the ground again.

"Aw, *Liverwurst!*" Everything was going wrong—
Wait. Calm down. That's no way to think.

It was not such a big deal after all, just a matter of getting the gate open and going in to catch him. And Colt would need to get the gate open anyway, to get Liverwurst out.

He maneuvered Bonita until she stood close alongside the gate, then backed her up until he could reach the sliding metal latch. "*Good* girl," he murmured to her. Maybe she was a little nervous about cars at this point, but she did at once what most horses for some reason would not do at all: She stood by the gate where he wanted her, and then stayed there while he struggled with the latch.

Which I can't seem to get open . . .

The latch was stiff. All the weight of the gate pulled down on it, making it bind. Mrs. Reynolds, when she opened it, lifted the gate with one hand and muscled the latch with the other, but Colt couldn't do that, not while keeping his balance on Bonita, who had to stand sideways to the gate in order for him to reach it at all. Colt set his teeth and grimaced, tugging on the latch handle as hard as he could without pulling himself out of the saddle. "You butthead!" he yelled at the latch, but it did not care. It would not move.

"Aw, *crud!*"

Once again he sat blinking back tears and trying to think. A person with legs that worked could walk right up to that gate and lift it and slide the latch open. . . . So what? Being handicapped just meant he had to do things differently—his way.

Under him Bonita stood patiently waiting.

Colt smiled. He lifted one of the lead ropes from his saddle and put a loop of it around the latch handle. The other end of it, halter and all, he hooked around the high pommel of his Spanish saddle. "Walk, Bonita," he ordered, signaling her with his seat.

The little horse was puzzled, feeling no contact on her reins. Hesitantly she took a few steps forward. The lead rope tightened, metal screeched against metal, the gate latch shot open, and the gate swung wide.

Liverwurst looked up and came trotting over, eager and interested.

"Good boy! C'mere, atta boy . . ." From Bonita's back Colt slipped the halter onto Liverwurst, snapped its throatlatch in place, and gathered the lead ropes into his right hand. "Good old Liverwurst. Come on, big guy. Let's go get Rosie."

Eagerly he sent Bonita up the farm lane.

He had to ride with only one hand on the reins, the left hand at that. No problem. Bonita did not seem to mind. Colt sent her into a medium-fast gait along the dirt road, because he wanted to get that stretch over with as quickly as possible. With Liverwurst's sizable body out almost in the middle of the road, he did not want to meet a car. So Bonita did a quick *paso corto,* and Liverwurst jogged along beside the little mare, apparently thrilled to be along for the ride. . . . Once he turned onto the state-park trail, Colt slowed the gait. No use taking unnecessary risks. Also, he wanted Liverwurst to calm down. It was going to be trouble enough getting Rosie on top of the gelding if Liverwurst behaved himself. If Liverwurst got happy and full of himself and acted like a jerk, it was going to be impossible.

Years later Colt still remembered that ride back to where he had left Rosie as the longest one ever. It seemed that way because he had to walk, it was safer to walk, helped the horses to be cool, calm, but it took so *long.* . . . There, ages later, finally, far ahead, was Rosie, still with his feet in the lake.

Rosie was shivering and looked around without enthusiasm as Colt rode up with Liverwurst in tow. "Oh, *maaan* . . ."

"There was nobody around," Colt explained. "This is the best I could do. Can you walk at all?"

With a groan and a grimace Rosie stumbled up. The icy lake water had numbed his feet for the time.

Bracing himself against trees, he was able to walk back to the trail.

"Okay. Now climb on something, a rock, a log . . ."

It was not too hard to find a suitable mounting block. Boulders and windfalls were everywhere. Rosie got on top of a large fallen trunk, and Colt led Liverwurst up beside it. Liverwurst, he noticed, did not maneuver as well as Bonita. Liverwurst did not want to stand as close to Rosie as was needed.

"Liverwurst!" Colt scolded, prodding the gelding in the side to make him move over.

"And you expect me to *ride* that?" Rosie complained.

"Just get on, Francine, before he moves."

"Shut up, Ozworth."

Unable to put all his weight on one foot, Rosie bellied onto Liverwurst and eventually managed to slither into riding position. Colt handed him the lead ropes by way of reins.

"Go slow," Rosie pleaded. "This animal is slippery."

They went very slowly. Colt knew Rosie would be hurting again soon. He did not want anything to joggle him. Just let Liverwurst nod along—

From just behind the trailside bushes a few feet away, three ducks flew up, splashing, quacking, clattering the reeds. Bonita scooted sideways and stood quivering. Liverwurst plodded on with scarcely a lift of his head.

"Hoo," said Rosie softly. "You all right, Colt?"

"Yeah." He urged Bonita forward and caught up with Rosie. "I'm starting to get used to that."

"This big guy is a good horse."

"Sure is."

"He's not much to look at, but he gets the job done."

"Sure."

Rosie's long legs hung down Liverwurst's warm, round, softly breathing barrel. With one hand Rosie stroked Liverwurst's wispy mane.

"He has about four or five different colors in his mane," Rosie remarked.

"That's Liverwurst," said Colt.

"When we get there," Colt instructed as they turned down the lane to Deep Meadows Farm, "you're going to have to ride Liverwurst into the stable aisle and get down on one of those boxes by the tack-room door. The phone is right inside the door. You should be able to reach it in a couple of steps. Heck, you can crawl to it if you have to." Colt had his plan all thought out.

But none of it was necessary. At the bottom of the lane they found cars everywhere. Mr. Reynolds was home, wondering where Liverwurst had strayed to. Some of the riders had arrived. And Colt's mother was there. She had called home to Lauri and then run out to the stable over her lunch hour, wondering what was taking Colt and Rosie so long. It seemed like half the world was there just waiting to help, now that Colt had done all the hard parts.

"I bet you were scared half to death," Colt's mother said to him after Mr. Reynolds had cut the seventy-dollar running shoes off Rosie with his jackknife and hurried the teenager away to the nearest emergency room, where Rosie's father would meet them. Audrey had to stay with Colt and help him put away Liverwurst and Bonita. As always when exciting things happened, she wanted to talk, and she chattered as she worked. "All alone with a situation like that to deal with. I bet you were petrified."

"Nope, Mom. I wasn't."

"Come on. This is your mother you're trying to kid. I've known you since you were a baby."

"I was upset," Colt said, "and mad, and worried about Rosie. But I wasn't really scared." And he felt a quiet joy, because he knew it was the truth.

He reached through the paddock gate, and patted Liverwurst and Bonita, and knew he could truthfully say one more thing.

"I don't get scared of things the way I used to, Mom. Not since I've been riding horses."

Chapter Ten

Just in time for Sunday dinner the next day Brad carefully wheeled Rosie in the front door. With one foot in a cast and the other ankle wrapped in an elastic bandage, Rosie was home to stay, but confined to a wheelchair for the time being.

"Boy, it's good to be out of that hospital!" Rosie looked around gratefully at the small, cluttered living room where his family smiled at him. "Where's Colt? Hey, Ozzie!" As Colt, who also happened to be in his wheelchair at the moment, rolled toward him. "Gimme a high five, hero!"

"Shut up." Colt blushed. Already he had heard enough "hero" stuff to last him the rest of his life. He had been mentioned on the late TV news the night before, and the phone had rung so much all day that his mother had disconnected it. The local

·COLT·

paper wanted to do an interview, but Audrey had vetoed that idea.

Colt rolled his wheelchair up beside Rosie's and gave him the requested victory salute. Muffins ran around in circles and barked with excitement. "You two guys watch you don't lock wheels," Lauri said.

"Wanna race?" Rosie offered. He struggled to get his wheelchair moving on his own. "Hey, Colt, give me some pointers on how to work this thing."

"Want to learn how to pop wheelies?"

Rosie was not ready for wheelies. Trying to thread the narrow path across the living room, he dodged Muffins, blundered into a pile of laundry, and got stuck. Everyone hurried to help him. "Oh, dear," Audrey sighed, looking around the crammed house. Magazines had cascaded off the coffee table onto the floor again, as always. Muffins had dragged in Lauri's old jump rope and left it coiled snakelike near the hassock. For some reason there was an open package of Rice Chex on top of the TV. "I am such a mess."

Colt said, "No, you're not, Mom." His mother had always taken care of him, talked to specialists, gotten him to his doctor appointments and his equipment fittings, seen that he took his medication, taken him to therapy, arranged for tutoring, attended conferences with his teachers, helped him with his homework, coached him through his exercises, made him learn to take care of himself, kept an eye on his shunt, bought braces and crutches and special shoes, and worked a full-time job to pay for everything. *And* made him brush his teeth and keep his nose clean and not swear more than was necessary. How could she keep calling herself a mess just because the house was a dump?

"You're not a mess, Mom. The house is a mess, so what?"

"I like it here," Rosie said, "mess and all. I don't see why you guys want to move."

Brad and Audrey stood still and looked at him. "You don't feel too crowded, sharing a room with Colt?"

"Not really."

"Me neither," said Colt. He liked having someone in his room to talk with and to play tricks on him. The night before, when Rosie had been kept at the hospital for observation and Colt was missing him, he had gone to bed to find his sheets full of potently perfumed talcum powder. Brad came in when he heard Colt laughing and had laughed with him. "Rosie told me to do that for him," he explained, and then he helped Colt change the sheets.

"*I* don't mind us tripping over each other all the time," Lauri said. "It's kind of fun." She and Colt had talked about this. Lauri had moved around so much in her life that she did not want to do it again, or not for a long time. And to Colt, having a big family, with a father and brother and sister, was all new. At first he had hated it. Now he couldn't get enough of it. He didn't mind being crowded.

"You know what I think?" Rosie said to his father and stepmother. "I think you guys ought to just stay here. And I know what you ought to do with all the money you've got saved up too."

"Oh, really?" Brad rolled his eyes at his wife, then looked back to his son. "Okay, lay it on us. I can't wait to hear this. What do you have in mind for our hard-earned money?"

Rosie said, "I think you ought to get some more horses. So we can all go riding with Colt."

There was a moment of total silence. Then everyone started talking at once.

Audrey to Brad: "You know, I really did enjoy riding Bonita."

Brad to Audrey: "It's a thought. It would be safer for Colt. Horses don't get so nervous when they're in a group."

"It's something we could all do together."

"And less hassle for Mrs. Reynolds, not to have Colt pestering her to take him out on the trail."

Colt to Rosie: "You really mean it? You'd get on a horse again? You sure you didn't hit your head?"

Rosie to anybody who would listen: "I just mean, like, real safe gentle horses. With cowboy saddles. None of that stuff where they make you go over jumps and wear tight pants."

Lauri, jumping up and down and clutching at the

adults: "Oh, oh, oh, a horse of my own, I can't believe it, oh, please, Daddy! Oh, please, Mom!"

And Brad and Audrey gave each other helpless looks and started to laugh. Which seemed to settle it.

"Tell you what," Colt told Lauri, businesslike, "suppose I take you out to the stable sometime and start giving you some riding lessons."

Colt told Mrs. Berry all about it the next time he saw her for physical therapy. "So as soon as Rosie is able to get around better, Mom and Brad are going to take a weekend and go out to Ohio to visit Mr. Ticknor and maybe buy some Paso Finos."

"Colt, that's wonderful." Bending over the padded table, measuring Colt for longer braces because he had grown so much, Mrs. Berry shook her head happily. She was, Colt noticed, a rather pretty lady, little blond mustache and all. "I'm so thrilled things are going well for you. And you know, I feel like I ought to take some personal credit. I'm the one who dragged you to Horseback Riding for the Handicapped, remember?"

Colt remembered, but Mrs. Berry didn't give him time to answer. She chattered eagerly on. "I can't believe how much you've grown up since then. It's hard to believe you're the same boy. You used to be such a—well, so immature."

Such a brat, she meant. Colt didn't know whether

to laugh or scream. "You noticed," he finally managed to say.

"I certainly did notice! You were quite a nui-
sance. Half the time I wanted to strangle you." Mrs.
Berry playfully put her hands around Colt's neck
and gave a gentle squeeze.

He grinned at her. "I'm glad you didn't."

"So am I." Mrs. Berry shifted her hands back to
her tape measure. "Now that you're feeling so much
stronger and surer of yourself, you've turned into a
beautiful human being."

Ick. But that was all right. Now that he had Bonita, Colt found it a lot easier to like life and everyone in it. Mrs. Berry and all her handicapped kids—
Anna Susanna, Jay Gee, Matt, cute little Julie.

Even boogerhead Neely, who was just coming in
the therapy-room door for his own session.

"Okay, Colt." Mrs. Berry helped him down off the
table onto the floor. "Fifty push-ups. Neely, you too."

"I can't do that many!" Neely whined.

Colt said, "Sure you can, Neely!"

"Drop dead!"

Colt didn't feel the least bit angry. Was that where
Mrs. Berry got her patience, just from feeling good
about herself? He said, "Hey, Neely, come on, you
got to try. I didn't used to think I could do it either."

"Butt out!"

"Neely," Mrs. Berry reproved, "Colt's just trying
to help. Push-ups, both of you. Start!"

Colt finished his fifty push-ups while Neely was still complaining his way through twenty. He wished he could make Neely see, make Neely understand. . . . He wished he could change Neely's life the way horses had changed his, because he knew exactly how Neely felt.

At the very back of his mind he decided that maybe he would help handicapped kids somehow when he grew up.

But meanwhile there were other things to do.

On a green-and-golden, blue-skied day in June, a family went horseback riding.

Up the Deep Meadows Farm lane, then along the dirt road. Mrs. Reynolds, now well and strong again, stopped the tractor she was driving and hollered after them, "Beautiful day!"

"Yeah!" Colt yelled back with the others.

"Have a good ride!"

"Okay!"

Brad's horse, the biggest one, was a sturdy chestnut gelding named Flame. He was not particularly handsome, but Audrey's little Maria del Consuela was a beauty. A *cremello*, a pale buckskin, lighter than Audrey's blond hair, with black legs and tail and a sunny streak in her long black mane—she was, Colt had to admit, almost as pretty as Bonita.

Lauri's horse was a flashy pinto Paso named *Luz*, "the light." Bonita liked Maria del Consuela, but did not get along as well with Luz. When Lauri let

·COLT·

Luz get her nose too close to Bonita's hindquarters, Bonita laid back her ears and lashed her tail, threatening. Colt sent her scooting forward before she could kick.

From Flame's back Brad glanced over at him. "Everything all right, Son?"

"Sure, Dad. I can handle her."

The adoption proceedings had begun. Colt would soon be officially a Flowers. When had he started calling his stepfather Dad? He couldn't remember. It had all been so natural, he hadn't noticed.

Into the state forest, onto the lakeside trail . . . Rosie rode up beside Colt, his long legs hanging well below his horse's belly. Rosie's horse? It was a big, homely, Roman-nosed, flop-eared Appaloosa with only the most pathetic excuses for mane and tail. Rosie rode Liverwurst, and loved him.

"Race ya," Rosie teased.

"Give me a break, Fran." Colt knew he would always be handicapped. He couldn't get reckless on horseback. Ever.

"Turkey! You know this snorting horsey of mine could beat you."

"Nothing can beat me," said Colt.